Praise for Annalisa Crawford

The Clock in My Mother's House

"Haunting, poignant, playful. Each one is a gem."
- Anne Goodwin, author of Matilda Windsor is Coming Home

"a haunting and wistful collection of short stories that will possess the reader's imagination long after the last page has been turned."
- J.S. Watts, author of the Witchlight series

Small Forgotten Moments

"A spellbinding, intoxicating journey into the dark heart of obsession. … another beautiful, heart-wrenching, epic masterpiece. I loved it."
Tom Gillespie, author of The Strange Book of Jacob Boyce

"A soulful tale of painting, secrets and longing, which draws the reader into a world of mystery and memory - an enchanting read."
Leonora Meriel, author of The Unity Game

"It's beguiling, haunting, beautifully paced and it kept me hooked to the very end."
Michael Walters, author of The Complex

Grace & Serenity

"The gripping story of a girl's downward spiral to the bottom. A FINALIST and highly recommended!"
The Wishing Shelf Book Awards

"The story of a desperate young woman who finds herself on a difficult path, and hurtles towards a thrilling conclusion. A tense and compelling read."
- Vikki Patis, author of In the Dark

Cat
& The
Dreamer

Also by Annalisa Crawford

ANNALISA CRAWFORD

Cat
& The
Dreamer

 Lynher Books

First edition 2012 Vagabondage Press
Second edition 2023 Lynher Books

Cover by: BookCoverZone

This book is dedicated to the
year 2012 – a challenging,
but important one

Contents

Me... Just Me

Today is Rachel's birthday. Born 17th November 1981. A bundle of joy, no doubt, for her doting parents who wrapped her in a fluffy pink blanket and brought her home in time for Christmas.

Fifteen years later, to that very day—to *this* very day—she was buried, right where I'm standing. Buried under years of untended grass and weeds, the plot neglected since her parents divorced and moved away; ripped apart, torn away. Shadows of grief are long and thriving.

The gravestone, once gleaming pale marble in the shape of an angel, is weathered with green moss, and tarnished with dirty rain; some of the lettering is starting to erode.

I hate that angel. I hate the way she smiles benevolently,

the way she stands prominent over the neighbouring graves, observing the cemetery with a smug, gloating expression. *Yes, I'm dead as well, but I'm still better than you.*

I toss the bouquet of lilac roses onto the grave without regard for presentation. The other plots have vases built into the base of the gravestone, or potted plants which are growing and flourishing. My pitiful offering is the only colour on this six-foot oblong. I kneel for my annual prayer: *dear Lord, thank you for saving me.* As the years pass, the more I think I should be admonishing Him for his failure to let me die as well.

The damp earth seeps through my jeans. I stand and check for grass stains. The wind rushes through the trees and I hug my coat tightly around me. My feet are rooted and I'm unable to muster the energy to leave.

I'm only going home, after all—there's nothing much for me there, aside from my mother preparing to dish up dinner and my father complaining about whatever news item has offended him today. I've tuned out his latest outbursts—gay marriage, single mothers, unemployed people sponging off his taxes. He has opinions on everything, and no one listens anymore.

In this small square of land, tucked between a housing estate and the dual carriageway, there's an otherworldly quality, a sense of timelessness. I catch the breeze; I float away.

The angel sneers at me as I turn and amble along the gravel path. I know she does.

When I walk through the front door, my parents are lying dead in the hallway. There are bloody trails along the carpet as if they struggled to escape the vicious attack or pleaded for mercy. I scan the scene for a moment, trying to absorb the truth of it

12

all, searching for clues. All I can truly think is: I'm an orphan.

In the living room, the furniture is overturned, the cushions are slashed; the drawers of the dresser open and the contents strewn across the floor. I crouch and graze my hand over the disarray. Nothing obvious is missing. The thieves—for there must have been more than one to assail two people at the same time—were looking for something specific. It appears my father's secret life as a spy has been compromised and curtailed.

When I walk through the front door, my mother is humming along to a song on the radio in the kitchen, pulling plates from the cupboard and rummaging in the drawers for cutlery. My father, unseen from my spot in the hall, will be inhabiting his customary place at the table, reading the newspaper and overlooking the fact he could be helping.

"Julia? Is that you?" Mum's voice cuts the air.

It would be such bliss, one day, to walk into the house and be alone, to move at my own pace, to take a bottle of cider from the fridge and open it while still wearing my coat. To not be required to speak. To enjoy the silence.

I consider ignoring her. I consider turning and running back down the street.

"Yes."

"You're late."

"I didn't go to work today, remember?"

"So, where have you been until this time?"

I shrug. Coat on its hook, bag slung over the banister. With all the other coats, with all the other bags.

"That bloody grave," Dad mumbles from behind the newspaper.

Mum looks from Dad to me. "Didn't you go this morning?"

This morning, this afternoon: the day is a blur.

"It's not good for you. Is it, Bev? It's not good for the girl." He leans back in his chair and raises his voice as if Mum's in another room.

"I'm not a child."

"Wandering off to that bloody cemetery all the time. It's best forgotten, that's what I say."

"It's not all the time. You know it's not all the time. And, I don't know about Mum, but I'm getting really fed up with hearing your opinions about it. Just let me be."

"Don't talk to your father like that."

"Like what?" I slump into the chair, arms folded defiantly across my chest, and wait for a plate to appear in front of me.

I'm fifteen years old again, being chastised for my perceived transgression. I slouch, visibly shrinking to inhabit the gangly, awkward body I left behind years ago. My head swarms with all the years I've not yet lived.

We eat in silence, because it's for the best, the way all our meals are eaten. Mum tries to make some effort—a remark about her day or the argument she overheard in the post office—before giving up and stabbing carrots with her fork. I nibble around the edges, not hungry. I'm never hungry when I come home in the evenings but Mum insists we sit together as a family.

Afterwards, I collect the plates, stack the dishwasher, wipe the sides, make coffee, and hide in my bedroom. And that's it: half-past six and my day has come to an end. No friends to meet for a drink, no evening yoga class, no date.

Pyjamas on, I scroll through endless TV channels for something interesting, then opt for a James Stewart DVD from my shelf. I've seen *The Philadelphia Story* so many times I know exactly what happens next; I deliver Katherine Hepburn's lines alongside her.

Despite my visit to the cemetery, I try not to dwell on Rachel, the girl who left, the girl who took so much of me with her. It rarely works; she's with me wherever I go, whatever I try to do. She's the glue keeping me stuck to my parents' house. When I close my eyes, she's right there in front of me, sitting on her bedroom floor, the glass in her hand.

The moon is bright when I turn off my light at half-past eight, casting silvery shadows around the room. There's a world of people out there who haven't even eaten dinner yet. They've returned from work and are sitting with a glass of wine beside their significant other to dissect the day, or they've taken their kids to an early cinema showing as a reward for good grades. They've considered cooking, but decided to eat at their favourite restaurant instead, because these people I've invented *have* a favourite. They have a choice of them. My parents go to a pub on the coast road, which they use for birthdays and anniversaries and random one-off celebrations. The rest of the time they—we—eat at home.

I fall asleep with the curtains open—staring at a sky which is sometimes moonlit and perforated with stars like tonight, sometimes shrouded with clouds—and every morning they're closed. Mum creeps in when I'm asleep and tidies around me as though I'm not there.

She folds my clothes, tucks my shoes under the bed in pairs, stacks the books which I've purposely left open and face-down because I can never find a bookmark. I've asked her not to, I've asked her to respect my space, but she curtly reminds me that this is her house and she's allowed in any room she likes, and I should remember that.

*

"This is really your life?" you ask, sitting on my bed and peering at my four walls with disdain. "This is really what you do every night, every single week? Just sit here and vegetate?"

"Yes, this is what I do. What did you expect? Extreme sports? An evening job as a lap-dancer?" I can challenge you because you aren't real right now.

"You've got posters on your wall like a kid." You stand in front of one. "I don't even know who that is."

Neither do I anymore. It's ripped and the face has faded in the sunlight; the sticky tape holding it up has yellowed. He's an actor maybe, or a drummer; denoting a time when my tastes veered towards long, dirty blond hair and a snarl.

You smile sadly and take both my hands in yours. "Poor Julia. Perhaps it's unfair of me to judge you. Why can't we be different and still get along?"

My words in your mouth. Oh Cat, why are you so understanding in my dreams and so ghastly the rest of the time?

That's you: you're Cat for this little romp. Because that's how I see you, as a shrewd and calculating cat. You're tall or short, always slim, brunette or blonde or auburn. Impeccably turned out, always having the perfect outfit for any occasion. You accumulate friends who know when to fade into the background and bestow you the limelight, who understand the consequences if they don't. Always snide and cutting. Always better than me.

You've been stalking me for years, assuming various guises. You were the PE teacher who singled me out in front of the entire class because I couldn't hit the baseball. You were the two snooty women at the make-up counter who ridiculed me when I bought my first eye-shadow aged seventeen. You were the bloke at my first job who drunkenly cornered me at the office Christmas party and spread vicious rumours I didn't understand when I panicked and ran away.

I know it's you, because you can't conceal your true nature, your soul. Your eyes betray you. Whenever we meet, as each of your incarnations worms its way into my life, you expose a brief, but unmistakeable, echo of the real you.

***

My parents leave for work before me in the morning. I remain in my room, eyes closed in case Mum chooses to check on me, until I hear the front door slam shut. Then I race to be ready in time—it can take as little as twelve and a half minutes from lying beneath my duvet to reaching the bus stop at the end of the road.

My lunchbox and flask are waiting for me in the kitchen as usual. Today, I leave them there. On purpose. I pause at the front door, and glance back with a twinge of doubt. My mother will take the rejection of her packed lunch to heart, which is melodramatic, yet precisely how she'll portray it. I'll have to lie to make amends—explaining how I overslept and didn't have time to pack my bag. It would be easier to just take it, but I don't. With the spectre of the lonesome plastic container in my mind, I force myself out of the house and into the stagnant drizzle.

In my world, drizzle doesn't exist. It's either hot and humid, causing cotton shirts to cling to sweat-sticky bodies; or heavy with thundering, driving rain; or infrequently, thigh-deep with soft snow you sink into as you walk.

Drizzle is ordinary. Drizzle is mundane.

The bus, when it finally arrives, winds back and forth across parallel roads, looping, swooping, descending aggressively on each stop as though utterly vexed it's expected to do so. The driver is prickly this morning. Each passenger is greeted with a grunt; and every passenger who hasn't immediately settled into a seat has been flung along the aisle as the bus jolts away.

At the crossroads, the driver takes a sharp left instead of carrying straight on. I glance out of the window to look for diversion signs or an accident ahead. Down Holborn Street, along River View… People follow my gaze out of the window; they murmur to each other. He's going the wrong way.

"Oi, mate, you're going the wrong way."

"Hey, this isn't the route. I'm going to be late for work. Let me off here, yeah."

"We're heading for the motorway."

"Stop him!" screeches one particularly hysterical woman.

The driver isn't listening. He's wearing headphones. swaying to the music. In the rear-view mirror, I recognise the serenity which envelops him as his plan develops and the desperate thoughts that besieged him begin to ease. I try to catch his eye, to smile and nod my acknowledgement: I've been there.

Around me, people are reaching for their mobiles. Phoning work to explain they'll be late. Phoning the police to tell them we've been kidnapped. Does anyone have the number for the bus depot? They flap and fizzle. They make plans to haul the driver from his seat and commandeer the bus. Does anyone know how to drive a bus?

I do nothing. I curl up against the window and settle in for the adventure. I doubt anyone would miss me if I didn't go into work today. I expect you, Cat, would have a few remarks to share with everyone. And later—when the bus is found burnt out with the charred remains of the suicidal driver and his thirteen passengers—you might feel a slight stab of guilt. A small stab. Maybe.

The bus stops because someone else presses the bell and I realise, as the passenger reaches the front, it's my stop as well. Or, to be accurate, the stop after my stop.

I meander to work; I'm going to be late. On purpose. I'm *always* on time, relentlessly reliable, that's me. When things need to be done, and no one else can be bothered: Julia will do it. So, no, today I'm going to be late.

Why, though? And why did I leave my lunch behind? Why did I fish out the vest with Little Miss Naughty on the front I got in the Secret Santa last year? Why did I keep it? Why am I wearing it? What's different about today?

The answer is nothing. Nothing is ever different.

"Oh Julia, I never realised," Andrew says, transcending time and space to be walking beside me, mid-conversation.

(The best thing about dreams is you can be mid-conversation without worrying how you got there.)

Andrew—my unrequited crush who worked in the corner shop one summer when I was thirteen—as clear in my mind as the last day I saw him.

"You weren't supposed to."

"I wish I'd known. I would have helped." He places his hand on my arm; the warmth of it makes me tingle.

"No one was supposed to."

"I would have been there for you."

Uh, yuck. Start again.

"I've never told anyone this before," I say, replaying the scene. It's a lie—I tell countless people in my head every day—but he won't know because I won't tell him. "My best friend died when I was fifteen. I didn't go to the funeral. I was in a coma. I woke up the day they buried her."

No, that's not right either. Andrew isn't the person to confide in; he existed too long ago, and he was too immature to have dealt with it. I imagine him married, with babies, with a dog, frazzled by work and mortgage payments, attempting to find time for a pint with a mate and failing. Too busy to care about the kid who used to hang around the magazine aisle and blush whenever he passed. Too long ago to remember me at all. The trouble is, I'm running out of people to tell.

The New Bloke

D ave, the boss, is deep in conversation with someone when I walk into the office. This *someone* has his back to the room, so I can only see the strain of his suit across his shoulders and a stray bit of hair which isn't combed straight. It must be the new guy—I'd forgotten he was starting today.

"So nice of you to join us," you say as I slide into my chair and switch on the computer. "And where were you yesterday? We had a pretty important meeting, if you didn't know."

You direct your voice towards Dave and grin at Karen and Manda, anticipating the trouble you'll be getting me into.

Dave's desk is in the far corner—close enough to hear without the need to increase your volume. He glances up and nods briefly at me, a *don't worry, it's fine* nod. We've spoken about it, in my rigid, limited fashion. He's aware there are days I need to myself, days I anticipate with trepidation but cannot explain why.

I assumed you'd have a dig—something bitchy and cutting, unable to stop yourself. But that contribution was remarkably muted. I follow your gaze to the new bloke. Ah, of course: got to make the right first impression, haven't you? No need to confirm your spitefulness too early, it might put him off.

"Right, folks." Dave stands, disregarding you, and your sneer falters. The other person stands as well and turns to face us. "This is Adam. Adam, this is the team: Cat, Karen, Manda, and Julia."

I blush because he's gorgeous, and that's what I do—I betray my feelings with my gaucheness.

Adam fidgets uncomfortably in his grey suit and first-day-shiny shoes. His hands are in his pockets, then clasped in front of him, then close to his chest while he twiddles a ring on his little finger. His dark eyes hold an uneasiness; his smile is brief. Not surprising, I suppose, with a room full of strangers directing their attention towards him, appraising him. He's chewing on his lip and avoiding too much eye contact, gazing towards the floor while Dave gives us a resume of Adam's previous experience and what he'll bring to the team.

He glances up and meets my eye. I fluster and look away.

You're happy, aren't you, Cat? You were keen for someone to flirt with. Your worst nightmare would have been another woman in the office, especially another woman like Christine who refused to be drawn into your gang and who, on occasion, took my side and left you smarting. So, you've got your toy, and when you've finished with him, you'll pass him on to Karen or Manda, and they'll have their fun as well. Poor man.

*

In my world, Adam would like the shy girl who sits quietly in the corner and avoids the chatter and merriment; the girl who works solidly, with her head down and hair falling about her face like a mask. He'd like the girl who doesn't care much for make-up and clothes, and whose beauty shines through nonetheless, with every smile or laugh. He'd find her mysterious and fascinating.

Dave asks me to take Adam through the basic duties, and you hate it—you were jostling to take him under your wing. I don't need to look to know you're glaring and making under-breath remarks to Karen while simultaneously smiling sweetly at Adam and offering silent commiserations that he's been lumbered with me.

Adam pulls the chair from his desk to sit beside me and waits for me to log in and fire up the correct programme. I run through a few of the easier tasks, explaining each step with uncontrollable stuttering, passing him the keyboard so he can repeat what I've just done. He moves closer to see the screen; I breathe in the scent of his aftershave and feel the warmth of his body. My heart is beating too fast, and my colour is rising.

"Have you been here long?" he asks when the computer freezes and I have no conversation to fill the gap. It occurs to me I should be the one asking questions: about his previous jobs, where he lives, his hobbies—small-talk to make him feel welcome, rather than the other way around.

"Ten years."

"Ten years? That's a long time. You never wanted to move on to something else?"

I shrug. "Never really thought about it."

"Never really good enough," comes your voice across the room.

I don't react. I busy myself with the computer, wiggling the mouse and bashing random buttons.

"Well," Adam says, "if someone enjoys their job, why move? There's more to life than chasing a career."

You snort. "She doesn't have much of a life either."

I sense his scrutiny in my peripheral vision and keep my head bowed to curtail his curiosity.

"Ah, it's working," he says enthusiastically as the computer leaps back to life, and we both focus on the screen again.

Occasionally, Adam's gaze strays to the side of my face, or to the back of my neck, as I reach for the correct folder from the shelf behind us. I struggle to keep my mind from wandering.

It's frustrating I couldn't maintain the pretence for a little longer, been intriguing and fascinating a couple more days. But maybe this is for the best. Everything restored to normal.

"Gotcha!" You stand behind me as I glance at Adam. "You can't have a boy like him. He's not going to look twice at you."

"Why not? You don't know anything about him. Or me, for that matter. You don't get to tell me what I can and can't do."

"You're sad and lonely, Julia, you project desperation," you say shaking your head ruefully and resting a hand on my shoulder. You lean forward and whisper, "Everyone knows you wouldn't know what to do with a boy if you got your hands on one."

"I've had boyfriends before."

"You're thirty and you've had two. And—really? You count Gavin?"

"I almost married Gavin."

"Yeah, until Mummy told you not to."

"It wasn't like that."

"Whatever. You're pathetic, and you always will be. Best leave Adam for me, eh?"

"Julia Summers," Adam says out of the blue the next day. Not a question, not a statement; but somewhere in between.

He's at his own desk now, working through a list of clients to add to the database. Has he been thinking about me all this time?

"I know you, don't I?"

I pretend to consider and feign interest in his musings. "I don't think so."

He stares and narrows his eyes. "Were you...? Did you...?"

My stomach clenches. I focus on my hands, palm-down on my desk, fingers spread evenly. I focus on my hands to prevent myself catching his eye and giving away how anxious I am—please don't say it, please don't say it.

He taps the end of his pen on the desk and shakes his head with a reflective frown. "Did you go to my school?"

It's what everyone ends up saying. If you know someone from *some*where, it must have been from school. Of course, you didn't recognise them at first, they've changed so much, and you've had so many friends it's hard to keep track of them all, isn't it? But, wow, you look great; how've you been?

He's not convinced, though, and continues to try and place me, glancing over when he thinks I'm not looking.

Please don't try too hard. Please don't.

People my age mostly remember, and they *do* remember, because of the shock. Not so much recalling the event itself, after all these years, but living with the consciousness of it tugging at them: they knew someone who did *that*.

There was an assembly at school, a memorial when I was still in hospital. Rachel had a bench in the foyer dedicated to her. Kids were sombre when they walked past it, dipping their heads or looking away.

But Adam didn't go to my school. He's from Nottingham, hundreds of miles away. Hundreds of miles away people heard about Rachel and me.

"Julia Summers," he murmurs, his interest waning. "I'm sure…"

I offer no clues, and after another glance across at me, he settles back to work; but I cannot.

You know, don't you Cat, the missing piece Adam's trying to find? You were there, egging me on. Or, at least, one of you was.

***

You call me Vomit Face behind my back. But I know, because you don't hide it—you latch on to the joke like a small child, repeating it incessantly. You scarcely contain it within gleeful whispers.

Don't you think she's far too skinny to be normal?

You used to call me Fatty at school, when my thighs chaffed in hot weather, and I got out of breath climbing the stairs to double science.

You delighted in picking me to be on your team (the first time, I was ecstatic—you liked me, *popular* girls got *picked*, everyone else was divvied up); then delighted in tripping me up with your hockey stick as I kept my eyes diligently on the ball, and yelling how useless I was.

You always find fault.

"We call her Vomit Face," you tell Adam with a giggle. Your voice floats across the room; you barely conceal it. "It's why she's so skinny—she eats, then she throws up, and she thinks we don't know."

But you don't know. Because I don't do it. The damage is done, though, because Adam eyes me suspiciously whenever I eat an apple or a chocolate biscuit in the office. I imagine him laughing along with the rest of you. Poor, stupid Julia; how glad we are that we're not like her.

I eat. I leave the room. I return. Maybe I look tired, a little red in the face.

It's a coincidence I read an email while eating a cheese salad sandwich and immediately have to visit Marketing along the corridor to clear up a confusion in person. When I come back, everyone looks up. You and Manda smirk; Karen stifles a giggle into the back of her hand.

"Told you," you stage-whisper, walking past Adam's desk and leaning down towards him. You lightly brush his finger, inviting him to share the joke. He pulls away.

In my world, Adam asks if I want to grab a coffee. He ushers me out of the office, his hand resting on my arm protectively, creating a distance, a barrier, between you and me. He looks back at you with a disapproving shake of his head, confirming his allegiance.

But all I can do, here in the office, with Adam avoiding my eye, with you and the others sniggering, is sit at my desk and try not to let a single tear escape. They're queuing up; my eyes sting and my cheeks burn.

In my world, when we leave the office for coffee, we don't come back for an hour. We talk, we laugh. We share silent moments and coy glances which leave me tingling. He listens to me as though I have something worthy to say. When we finally return, he's holding my hand because it feels right.

"I need those figures by the end of the day," Dave says, patting my desk to catch my attention and breaking into the dream. I close my fist, clutching an illusory hand.

A Perfect Dream

When you catch the same bus every day, you're aware of the same people travelling along with you—the same weary faces going the same weary way. You recognise them in the department stores where they work, or the coffee shops where they buy lunch or a relaxing post-work latte. You nod politely and wonder if they recognise you too. Perhaps not. Perhaps you're just a smudge in their peripheral vision. You become accustomed to their tickly coughs, and the way they sigh as they settle into the seat or mime to the song they're listening to, emitting inadvertent murmurs. When they're not at the bus stop on time, you worry.

You know particular things about them, such as where they get their hair done and how many times their mum has been married, simply by listening to one-sided phone conversations. You know how much they owe the bank by glancing down at the letter in their hands when you should be facing firmly forwards. You fill in other details—unfaithful partners, unruly kids, a penchant for ballroom dancing—to break the tedium.

"Why are you still living with your parents?" asks the guy sitting across the aisle from me. He's always in that seat in the afternoon, playing Solitaire on his phone. Sometimes when I edge past, he looks up. It's almost a relationship.

"It's complicated…"

"How?"

"Oh, the usual. Money, time, you know."

"I think there's more to it."

"Well, there always is, isn't there?" I sigh, cornered, and lean towards him. "They don't trust me. I'm thirty years old and they don't think I can handle living by myself."

"You don't need to ask permission. You just go home and say you're moving out. You could do it today."

"They'd freak. Well, Mum would; I don't know about Dad." I pause. "I used to be close to him, but—well, we grew apart. These things happen, I guess."

Moving out, living alone—could I? A silent house when I came home, a cider waiting in the fridge…

"Fathers always love their daughters. He'd miss you, but he'd know it was right."

"I did a bad thing," I whisper conspiratorially, "and he doesn't love me anymore."

"A bad thing?" He watches me intently as I shuffle in my seat. I shiver under the scrutiny.

"I tried to… I… My friend…"

*

It's gone. The illusion is broken up, scattered around the bus. The chatter invades my space; the revving engine grates. The drizzle, grey and hazy, clings to the window.

My dreams are always vivid, lurid almost, like an over-exposed photo. It's how I know what's real. Reality is tinted with a disappointing grey pallor, washed out, even when the sun is shining and the sky is cobalt blue, or golden leaves are falling from the trees. It's how I know this bus is real, this journey is real, this life is real.

***

Days pass quickly when you're not paying attention. Friday arrives—the end of Adam's first week. He's settled in well and keeps his distance from you, which you choose to interpret as him biding his time before asking you out. I note his exchanges with you are polite and not overly intimate. He stands with one foot in front to prevent you coming closer. I wonder where your assertion comes from.

"I've seen the way he looks at me," you told Karen on his third day. "You've seen it too—I know you have. It's so obvious. I bet he'll take me somewhere really classy, don't you?"

Yet, he hasn't, has he? I don't gloat, or smirk, as you would. At least, not to your face.

"Can you check this email is okay?" Adam asks. We're alone in the office so he must be talking to me. I cross to his desk, and he stands so I can take his seat. "Coffee?"

"Yes, please." I read the words on the screen. "This is fine. You honestly shouldn't worry—you're doing a great job so far." And, as always, I blush a little; I hope he's starting not to notice.

He flicks the switch on the kettle and spoons coffee into mugs.

He turns and leans against the filing cabinet with his hands in his pockets. Casually sexy. Sexily casual. "All thanks to you."

It's my turn to speak, to say something which will prolong the conversation, to make him think I want to speak to him. A *you're welcome*. Anything. The pause becomes a crevice.

"Oh, perfect timing. I could do with a coffee." You burst into the room, Manda and Karen following like ducklings. "We've had the most *boring* meeting ever. You should be glad, Julia, that you don't have to bother with this kind of thing in your role."

"And me," Adam agrees, standing straighter and losing his smile. "You make it sound awful."

"Oh, no, you'd be amazing. You're the type of person this place needs. Drop the deadweight and get some proper talent in. You'll be up for promotion in no time." You cast your eyes briefly in my direction; Adam's eyes follow instinctively.

I can't recover from your contempt, so I return to my desk and disappear. I watch, without meaning to, as Adam pours water into two mugs. I notice the defined muscle across his shoulders and back as his shirt tightens when he moves. I sigh, without meaning to, as I imagine my arms around his neck and his torso pressed into mine. The colour is rising in my cheeks.

He puts a mug on the corner of my desk, his hand hovering until I glance up and thank him. He grins and shakes his head, rolling his eyes towards you, Cat. Or am I mistaken? I suppress a giggle.

"Where's mine?" you demand with a flutter and a pout. You laugh, you think it's a game. You don't understand.

"Sorry. There was only enough water for us." He sits without any offer to make you one, and I think I love him.

"Oh, I almost forgot, Adam," you say, desperate to cling on to the conversation. "We usually pop to the pub after work on a Friday. Come along. I'll buy you a pint to celebrate your first week."

"You *all* go?" He looks at me in surprise.

"Well, Julia's usually got something else on... The rest of us, though—"

"You don't go?" Still looking at me, his voice a little softer.

I shake my head. "No, not my thing, not really."

He turns back to you. "And I'm busy tonight, sorry. Maybe next week. Maybe Julia will be free then too." And no one really knows how to reply, least of all you, Cat.

***

It drizzles, then it rains. I get damp, then I get drenched. I hide beneath the hood of my coat and peer through the downpour, staring miserably at the stream of headlights coming towards me. Not one of them is my bus. I shiver as rain batters against me and my skirt clings to my legs.

I've been here fifteen minutes, and all I want is to go home, take a hot shower, and imagine all the things a normal person would be doing on a Friday night.

"Need a lift?" Adam pulls up at the kerb.

"I'm fine." I lower my head. Even in my dream, I'm reticent and bashful.

"You're soaked!" He dashes around to me, opens the passenger door, and ushers me in. "I'm not leaving you out here

like this." He runs back around and launches himself into the driver's side. "Ugh. Right, where to?"

I hesitate. I picture Mum's face if a strange man dropped me outside the house. I'd have the third degree all night.

He rests his hand on mine. "Why don't you come to mine? You look like you need someone to take care of you for a while. Do you fancy a pizza or something?"

Adam's house is freezing. (No, there's no journey in a dream!) *He closes the curtains and switches on two lamps which cast an orange glow across the room. He kneels at the hearth and makes fire appear as if by magic. I wait by the door with my coat on and rainwater dripping from my fringe and down my neck.*

"Oh, I'm sorry. I'll find you a towel. I've got a dressing gown somewhere you can use. You shouldn't be in those wet clothes." He holds my gaze a moment too long, then takes my coat and leaves the room.

I sit in front of the fire, leaning against an armchair, and wait for the first wave of heat to hit me. Yellow flames dance in the draught; wood crackles gently. For once, I'm completely relaxed, totally calm. I don't notice Adam come back until he sits on the chair behind me and wraps the towel around my shoulders. He scoops up my hair and smooths it dry; he pulls stray tendrils away from my face. All without a word. All with the gentlest of touches.

I turn to see the soft smile hovering on his lips, his gaze sincere and tender. And I kiss him. I pull back in shock, but his hand is on the back of my head, drawing me towards him. He kisses me again, long and slow and lingering. He slips from the chair to the floor, brushing his cheek against mine, kissing my neck.

His hand wanders down my arm and he pulls my jumper over my head and unbuttons my shirt agonisingly slowly. He smiles at the Little Miss Naughty vest I'm wearing beneath it, raising his eyebrows and asking, "How naughty, exactly?"

"Very naughty."

Where would I have ended up if my life had been different? Not here. I could have done anything, gone anywhere.

One moment of recklessness and everything was changed forever.

Twenty minutes, still no bus.

Maybe I should walk to a different stop, make some effort. Suddenly it all seems too much. Suddenly I want to sink to my knees and let salty tears cascade down my face.

My Best Friend, Rachel

I met Rachel in maths. She was new, standing at the front of the class, flanked by Miss Potts, the maths teacher, and Mr Hughes, the Head. Rachel surveyed the room with indifference. If it was me, I'd have been mortified having everyone staring like that.

"Class, this is Rachel Carr. She's moved here from Taunton. I hope you'll make her feel welcome." Miss Potts turned to usher her further into the room with a rare smile. "Take a seat, Rachel. Look, there's one next to Julia."

I'd been trying to make the desk next to me appear occupied by spreading out my books. It didn't work and Rachel stood beside it until I moved my bag from the chair to the floor. She slipped beside me wordlessly and stared at the blackboard.

She sat tall in the seat, like a model, head up and shoulders back, a detached expression on her face as if this class and everything was beneath her.

She rolled her pen between her fingers and the desk, making an irritating, grinding sound; her book—frustratingly—was open at the wrong page. I envisioned my hand sweeping across to snatch the pen away from her. Or reaching over and turning the page to the correct one. The more I watched her fingers rolling the pen, the more annoyed I became, the louder it was, the more distinctly I saw myself doing it. Suddenly, I grabbed the pen and we both stared at my hand in shock.

"Sorry," I mumbled, trying to make it sound as least like an apology as possible.

"S'awright," she replied, equally unintelligibly.

"Julia," called Miss Potts harshly, and I jumped slightly in my seat. "For the second time"—pausing for the flow of jeers around the room—"can you tell me the answer to 3b on page 34?"

Fractions. My worst topic. I liked algebra—I understood why letters might replace numbers and the way you could figure out what number was missing. It was a puzzle, a challenge. But we'd done algebra. This term was fractions.

Why would I care what 5/6ths plus 5/8ths equals? How often would I need to make that calculation?

I flustered, colouring deeply and wishing myself a long way from the classroom and the gawking eyes waiting for me to fail. Miss Potts asked the question again, knowing I didn't know. She spoke very slowly and carefully, causing more hilarity among my classmates.

"Fatty doesn't know," someone muttered from behind their textbook. "The Big Fatso can't answer it." Few people heard, but those who did sniggered and turned their heads. I sank into my chair and forgot the question entirely.

Rachel, who'd been sitting primly, ignoring the fuss around her, pushed her exercise book towards me and tapped my arm to draw my attention to her ornate writing in the top corner. The answer! Or, maybe *not* the answer, maybe anything but that, to fit in with the others.

It was all I had though. "One and 11/24ths?"

Miss Potts eyed me suspiciously, her lips pursed. "Correct." How she hated saying that. Then turned away. "Alison…"

I smiled at Rachel, but she turned away as well, bored again. What I noticed afterwards was that there were no workings out on the page. Only the answer. Miss Potts always said the workings out were just as important as the solution itself.

The bell rang. I gathered my books and pushed them into my bag, taking my time so I'd be the last one out. The boys used to wait for me in the corridor sometimes, to push me over or to up-tip my bag so the contents spilled across the floor. The longer I took, the more fed up they'd become of waiting.

That day, though, it was Rachel leaning against the wall opposite with her arms folded. "Miss Potts says you can show me where to go next. You're in my French class, too."

"Oh." I fussed with my bag and avoided her gaze. "Turn right at the end of the corridor. Follow the girl with the pink bag, she's in the same class."

I didn't move. I always arrived last to make sure everyone was seated, and the teacher was over-seeing my every step.

Rachel started to walk away, then stopped and whispered, "I was bullied too. At my last school. It's why we moved. I know what it's like."

"You moved a hundred miles because you were bullied?"

"Sort of. But, if you want to talk… that's all…"

"Why? Why were you bullied, I mean?"

"Because I'm clever," she said without conceit. "I was taking A-Level Maths two years' early. I'm not anymore. My parents thought it would happen again if I continued with it. So, I'm taking my GCSE again, which is pointless." She stabbed her heel against the wall.

It was my turn to say something. I blushed before I spoke. "I'm stupid. And fat and slow and ugly."

"Oh." She hesitated, smiling almost compassionately, then followed the girl with the pink bag.

I don't remember becoming friends with Rachel. But I did, sort of, and quickly. She was dead three weeks later, so it had to have been very quick.

The first time I began to worry about Rachel we were in my bedroom listening to Madonna. She'd been quiet for a while, half-heartedly humming along to the songs. We were lying on my bed and staring at the ceiling. Every so often she raised her legs so they were straight up and wiggled her toes.

"My aunt killed herself," Rachel said.

"When?" I lifted my head, expecting her to be gripped with grief-filled tears.

"Last year."

"Oh. I thought you meant now."

I was surprised to be disappointed. Perhaps I was imagining a funeral, with the mourners wearing dramatic black, and being a supportive shoulder for her to cry on so all her family would love me. I can't remember.

We fell silent and the CD finished. Mum's voice floated up the stairs—she was on the phone to someone, cheerful and light, falsely friendly.

"How did she kill herself?" I flipped over onto my stomach and propped myself up on my elbows.

"Most people ask why."

"Well, that's obvious—she didn't want to be here anymore."

Rachel snorted. "I suppose." A pause; a deep breath. "She drowned. Left her clothes on a rock at the beach and walked into the sea. She never came out. She kept walking knowing it was going to get too deep at some point. Can you imagine? Being desperate enough to keep walking? It's why we moved. There were too many horrible memories back home."

"You're making it up. You've got loads of reasons for why you moved. I bet your dad just got a new job and you're trying to make it more exciting."

"How do you know it's not the real reason and I've made up all the others because it's too hard to think about?" She screwed her mouth into a tight knot, like I'd seen her mum do.

I lay back down, not having a clever way to answer. Although she was my friend now, although I'd never want to hurt or upset her, sometimes she made me feel as stupid as the bullies at school did. Sometimes, when she was like that, I hated her too.

"Did she leave a note?" I asked, going back to the beginning.

"Yes. Mum and Dad tried to hide it from me. They tried to tell me she died in a car crash."

"How do you know she didn't?"

"Because I read about it in the paper."

"That's awful."

"I found her suicide note when I was looking for my birthday presents. They'd kept it—can you believe it? Like a souvenir or something." Her eyes glazed over, until she shook her head and refocused. "I don't see the point of notes. I don't think I'd write one. People want to put the blame on someone else when they do it. My aunt said she couldn't cope with my dad being happier than she was, that she'd always felt she was in his shadow. Don't you think that's cruel, to lay so much guilt on someone? He loved her so much, and she said that about him."

"I don't know. I'd probably blame everyone who calls me names for being fat and laughs at me in PE. Yeah, I'd name them all and curse them, for good measure. I'd wish them all to have kids who can't catch a ball or climb a stupid rope."

The next day, Rachel wasn't in school. Or the one after that. I'd only known her two weeks by then, but I was vulnerable without her beside me in class or walking around the playground with me at lunchtime. I crept along corridors between lessons, reverting to my previous tactics to remain undetected because she wasn't there to ward off the taunts and teasing. My long-standing nicknames made a comeback, like ghostly echoes.

In the toilets, I heard a rumour she'd slashed her wrists and was in hospital. Someone else said they were told she'd been surrounded by a gang after school and beaten so badly her parents didn't recognise her. When I came out of the cubicle, they looked guilty for a second, then laughed and ran out.

I almost hugged her when she returned to school. But I didn't; I shrank back from her instead. She was different. Her eyes were sad and angry; her whole body was deflated. In her favourite lessons, she didn't call out the answers like she normally did. She was silent and sullen, and when I asked her what was wrong, she stared with derision and walked away.

I furtively checked her wrists. I asked her to reach for my coat and examined her skin as her sleeves rode up—maybe not so furtive, after all. There were no cuts, no bruises either. And I was worried.

"What do you think it feels like when you die?" she asked one day during our lunch break. She was doodling on a blank page at the back of her English textbook. "You know, afterwards, in heaven?"

"I've never thought about it."

"I bet it's wonderful. Lots of colour and music and laughter, and all the people who've already died are waiting for you."

"Like your aunt?"

"Yes, like my aunt. Don't you think?"

"Um, yeah, if you believe in that kind of thing."

I'd never considered heaven a satisfactory idea. I'd never been to church regularly. Mum dragged me along on a whim sometimes, to impress a new friend, perhaps, or if she'd been to a good funeral. We'd wake up early on a Sunday morning, dress in our smartest clothes, and walk two miles to church because my father—who normally drove us to places—wouldn't get involved in these schemes. We'd do it for a month or two, then she'd get bored, and I'd be released from my duty until the next time.

"What do you believe, then?" Rachel pressed, closing the book and leaning forward solemnly.

"I believe," I said slowly, not used to people asking my opinion on things; unsure I even *had* an opinion on this, "when you die, that's it. You close your eyes and go to sleep, and you don't wake up. There's no afterwards, no perfect heaven. You just go to sleep and don't dream, and you do that forever."

"Oh." She was silent, staring at a money spider crawling across her shoe, moving her foot to keep it elevated off the floor. "No, it can't be." She shook her head. "It can't be like that." She folded her arms across her body as if suddenly cold. "No, that's not right. There has to be something more."

***

I guess Rachel ran all the way to my house; she was bright red and panting when she burst into my bedroom and flung herself on my bed without a word. I briefly wondered what Mum, who must have let her in, would be thinking about this strange new friend of mine. I imagined the type of probing I'd have to endure later.

Rachel buried her face in my duvet and sobbed, her body trembling. Tentatively, I tapped her shoulder. She pushed me away.

Eventually, she looked up, bemused, as if not sure how she had ended up in my bedroom. "I want to die."

I was used to it by now—to these extremes of emotion: to Rachel's flamboyant laments and brooding despair—but this was nothing I'd seen before.

"What's happened?"

"I hate them."

"Who?"

In my head I listed the people who may have provoked this reaction: her parents, girls at school, the boy next door who she had a crush on.

"Everyone."

"Let's go and have some cake. Mum's been baking."

"Oh, for God's sake, Julia, don't you think you're fat enough already?"

"I—that's not—that's really cruel." I tried not to cry, to blink back the tears. "I thought you were my friend."

"Grow up, Julia. No one has *friends*. We're all miserable, lonely creatures shitting on everyone else."

I recoiled.

She smiled, half-smiled, revealed the merest hint of a smile. "But it's okay, because I've got a plan."

"What plan?" I was annoyed with her but curious.

She looked startled for a second. Wide-eyed. "No, nothing. There's no plan. I was just…"

"You said you had a plan. Don't you trust me?"

"Don't you trust me?" she mimicked harshly. "I'm sorry. Forget it, it's nothing." She chewed the skin around her finger-nail, quiet and diminished.

It occurred to me I'd never known which one was the real Rachel. I'd so desperately wanted a friend, I grabbed hold of the first person who was anywhere near nice to me.

Was I one of the people she hated?

"It's nothing. I'm nothing. I want to die." Her voice was tiny, pensive. "I'm going to."

"You're not serious. Tell me you're not serious."

Her face fell. Her eyes were wide like a little rabbit. Maybe she really hadn't meant to tell me; or maybe by saying it out loud it was tangible and real and there was no going back.

"Forget it. Forget I said anything." She curled herself back into a ball on my bed and hugged my pillow.

What was I supposed to do now? Should I tell someone? My mother? Hers? It was too big for me to deal with, but I had no idea how Mum would react. She'd forbid me seeing Rachel, dismiss her as a trouble-maker she didn't want me getting caught up with.

"But, what about your parents? They love you. What about me? Think of all the things you can do when you're older. It's not always going to be as crap as this. In couple of years, we'll leave school and do whatever we want. Surely that's worth waiting for."

"You think so?" She sat up again, and looked at me earnestly, ready—it seemed—to believe any lie I was willing to tell.

I held my head straight. I kept my gaze steady and even.

"What do you think heaven is like?"

"Oh Rachel, I don't know."

We sat there for a long time. Rachel stared out of the window, a faint smile on her lips as she, presumably, imagined a heaven that could never really exist.

Rachel's sadness lingered. It didn't go away as I'd hoped. She grew smaller, hunched, distant. She picked at her lunch, sat silently in lessons, allowed any number of insults to fly over her without retaliation, as if she hadn't noticed them, or they no longer mattered.

"Come with me," she said. It was a Friday, after school, in my bedroom or hers. Outside, it was grey with drizzle.

"Where?"

She didn't answer, but I knew. "No."

"Why?" she spat. "What have you got here?"

"Do you ever wake up and dread the whole day?"

"No."

But I did.

I dreaded the sniggering as I walked past groups of girls from the year below, trying not to notice the way they waddled behind me, imitating me. Trying to ignore the rumours about me. The sneering, the whispering. Condoms tucked between the pages of my textbooks that spilled over my desk when I opened them.

"Do you ever wake up in the morning and feel exhausted that you have to go through another day?"

"No."

But I did.

I'd lie in bed as long as I could before Mum yelled up the stairs that I was going to be late again, disappointed the world hadn't ended overnight, frustrated I didn't own a time machine to take me to a future where I'd be a successful adult living a wonderful life, and all the bullies would have their comeuppance.

I'd sit at the table, unable to force down the cereal I'd poured, unable to leave the house, laden with so much distress.

"Do you ever wake up in the morning and wish you hadn't?"

Yes.

But how could I admit it to a girl I'd only known for three weeks?

"Come with me?"

"Yes."

Rachel. A girl I barely knew—my best friend—shaped the life I lead; continues to do it even now, like persistently restyling plasticine, the structural integrity becoming less assured the longer it's messed with. I'm drawn to her grave every year, reliving the funeral I couldn't attend. Stuck in time.

In my world, I am a fifteen-year-old girl, trying to hold onto the first friend I'd ever had.

She'd have made a better job of being alive than me. The shock of finding me dead beside her would have focused her, made her want to embrace the reprieve she'd been given.

Why didn't I die? Not so many pills, not so much of that horrid cheap rum slugged down. Not so much of a desire to do it. Rachel *needed* to die; she needed to know what it felt like, needed to gasp those final breaths.

Switched off in her sleep, a teddy bear at her side, dressed in pretty pink pyjamas.

I'm a fifteen-year-old girl waiting to grow up, waiting for my life to start, to exorcise the ghosts. There was no reason for either of us to die, but we both did, in our own way.

***

We didn't go to school, that morning. We left our houses like it was any normal day, bags packed with history and science books. We walked around the block, idling away the time, kicking Coke cans along the pavement, and once Rachel's mum had left for work, we went back to her house.

I regret we went there. It was a mistake. But it was Rachel's plan, I was only a passenger. She'd been stashing aspirin and her mother's sleeping pills in the bottom of her drawer for weeks; she'd acquired the alcohol. Weeks! I'd only known her three. This plan was older than our friendship.

There was never a moment I questioned what we were about to do. We'd discussed it, planned it like it was a normal Friday night sleepover or something; each detail mapped out. Now, we were watching ourselves carrying out the plan. It wasn't real. At no point did I believe tomorrow wouldn't happen.

Rachel poured the rum into plastic beakers. I'd never had alcohol before, not even a glass of wine at Christmas. I held it, sniffed it.

"One, two, three, go." We drank together, coughing as it hit the back of our throats. It was repulsive, tasting like medicine.

Rachel drained her glass and poured another. I struggled with the first.

"Here, now these." She handed me some sleeping pills. Eight little blue tablets. I nestled them in my palm, pushing them with my finger. Rachel caught my eye, and for the first time, seemed uncertain. She stared at the tablets in her hand then ate them all up.

"I hope Mum doesn't find us," she said at one point. "I hope it's Dad. He'll know what to do. I don't want Mum to find us."

Suddenly it was real. I hesitated over the aspirin—I didn't want anyone to have to find us, I didn't want someone turning up on my parents' doorstep to tell them what had happened.

"Julia, you're not taking enough. You have to swallow more, or it won't work."

"I can't. My throat hurts." *And I'm scared. I'm so scared.*

"Then have a drink. Don't leave me."

I saw the desperation in her eyes.

"Think what they'll say in school. No one will laugh at us ever again."

I remember thinking we were cool now. We were bunking off school and getting drunk. We fitted in, finally!

I wanted to tell Rachel that; I wanted to suggest we should

stop this; we should go to school and get caught paralytic in the playground. We'd be cool. Our parents would be furious and I, at least, would be grounded forever—but we'd be alive, still alive.

"Just remember every cruel comment anyone ever made to you," she was saying. I must have blanked out for a moment. "All those girls who laughed when you split your shorts in PE or fell over in the mud in cross-country. Or couldn't catch the ball."

Her words slurred; spaces elongated between them. She was crying. She took another sip and slumped against the bed. "You're the only friend I've ever had. I'm going to miss you."

"I'll miss you too. And chocolate cake."

She laughed. "Me and chocolate cake? Is that all?"

"What about you?"

She was thoughtful for a moment. It seemed like a long time but the second hand on the clock barely moved. "Nothing." She wiped a tear from her cheek and smiled sadly. "Not having children, I guess. Getting married in a beautiful white dress and having someone look at me as though I'm the best thing in the world."

That was the last thing I heard her say. One of us fell asleep; I can't remember who went first.

You weren't always Cat. You were once as real as I am, born and living in one body; trapped, I suppose. Perhaps you were always searching for an escape, for something better. You seem to have fun as a spirit, flitting in and out of other people, tormenting me because I lived.

You had parents. You had a birthday. You had a death day.

You had a name. You were Rachel.

Do you remember? Can you remember who you were? I can. I can't forget.

Me... Again

"*Then* what happened?"

"Uh?"

I'm walking along a windy cliff top, no idea where, clinging to a strong firm hand. I don't look up, so I don't know who the hand belongs to. I look down instead—to my feet navigating slippery rocks and muddy puddles, to the steep drop on our right where the path has crumbled, becoming unstable and jagged. I'm drawn to the edge, creeping closer and closer. I'm ready to jump. I want to jump.

But the hand grips mine and eases me away. He—definitely he—wraps his arm around me until the desire diminishes.

"Then what happened?" he repeats.

Waves crash against rocks; the noise thunders around us.

"I woke up." What else is there to say? "I expected to be dead, but I woke up."

I'm empty, torn apart. Why am I here, forcing myself to go over this again?

"Rachel was. She was dead, I mean. They told me later, when they decided I was strong enough to hear it. But I'd already worked it out. I kept asking to see her, and they fobbed me off with some stupid excuse."

I am a fifteen-year-old girl trying to understand. But really, I don't have a clue.

"And then?"

"There is no, and then. There's just this, right now."

I look at him for the first time. I'd expected him to have a face by now, become somebody I recognise, but my imagination has forsaken me. I stare at this unknown figure, and I don't have the words.

"Leave me alone," I whisper. "Please leave me alone."

I gaze out of the window without seeing the view beyond. Our office is on the second floor, slightly higher than the cliff in my dream. *I'm out on the ledge, taking a step—*

"God, is she still comatose?" I hear you say from a long way off.

"Shut up," Adam hisses. Or does he?

"Are you coming for lunch, Adam? Coffees on me."

"Er, no, I'll stay... I've got some work I want to... I brought sandwiches."

There's a pause, then the door slams shut.

I jump. Am I alone?

"Julia? Are you okay?"

No, not alone. I exit the orange glow of my daydream and

turn to Adam, who's regarding me with such concern. Concern? Really? Maybe not; maybe with curiosity. Or I *am* a curiosity: a time bomb, an explosion that hasn't happened yet.

"Sorry, I was miles away. I'm—I'm not sure I'm feeling too good, I might just…" Just what? My head spins, a wave of nausea rises. Am I ill and need to go home?

"I think you could do with some fresh air. Fancy a walk?" He glances out of the window. "It's stopped raining."

I don't know what to say—my instinct is to say no, to hide away at my desk, like I usually do.

"We won't be long."

"Okay," I say in a voice which doesn't sound like mine.

"I was lonely," I say to the man who won't leave me alone, the stranger with no face who feels so safe and compassionate. "You asked me, and then?" I remind him.

He nods. "I did."

"I'd never really felt alone, even before Rachel. But once she was there, and then so suddenly not *there, I was scared. When I walked into school for the first time after it happened—a long time afterwards, maybe three or four months—everyone just watched me. There were eyes everywhere, waiting for me to do something absurd or irrational. They didn't bully me anymore, they simply didn't do anything."*

I sneak another glance to see who I'm talking to, and still, there's no face.

"I'm not good with people, I probably ought to be alone."

"You don't get along with the others, do you?" Adam asks, as though making some great revelation.

"You noticed? What gave it away? The stony silences, or the

icy stares? The bitchy nicknames, maybe?" It's colder than I thought it was going to be; I left my gloves in the office. I tuck my hands inside the sleeves of my jacket.

"The way you seem much happier when they're not around."

"Ah, yes. I'm not as good at hiding my feelings as I'd like to be."

"It's not always a good thing. Some people might… like to know how you're feeling."

I don't know how to reply so I stare at the pavement ahead and wonder how far we'll be going.

Conversations never drift away when I'm involved; they shudder to a halt. I sense that's what's happening now, and how Adam is probably regretting his act of altruism. We're stuck for the length of time it'll take to walk back. In the office, I could find a distraction, search for a pen in my desk drawer or 'fix' a problem with the printer. Here, I'm exposed, and the silence—*my* silence—is awkward and oppressive.

"So, you've worked here ten years?"

"Yes."

"Haven't you ever wanted a change? I mean, it's an okay job, but it's not a career."

"It doesn't seem that long, to be fair. I'm—"

"Stuck?"

"Settled."

He grins. "What did you want to be when you were at school?"

I freeze. School? I wanted to be nothing at school. Quite simply nothing.

"I don't remember."

"I wanted to be a vet. But, as it turns out, I… faint… at the sight of blood."

56

I laugh then cover my mouth aghast. "I'm so sorry. I didn't mean to laugh." I blush deeply and the horror trickles into my stomach. Laughing at people is mean—I should know.

"It's okay, it is funny. I was about eight—it wasn't a long-held dream or anything."

We smile at each other until it feels strange, then look ahead again. I focus on my breathing, on each step, on the fog lifting from my head. I wonder if, had he discovered Manda or even Cat looking upset, he would be here with them instead of me.

"We should probably turn back," he says, and I find myself disappointed. We pivot and he's on my right now, like the man in my daydream. "Okay, so not work. What about... holidays? What's been your favourite place to visit?"

"Um." I shake my head with an apologetic grimace.

I *have* been on holiday. Belgium once, Guernsey too. But I was with Mum and Dad, so it doesn't really count. I've never thought about going away by myself—how weird it would be to choose to eat alone in a restaurant, or explore a city without someone there to make sure I didn't get lost. I shake my head again and see myself as Adam must be seeing me. He'll be so relieved to get to the office with normal people again.

"Let's go somewhere right now," Adam says, stopping abruptly in the middle of the pavement. He leans in close and whispers, "Let's go somewhere hot and sultry, anywhere you want. We'll go to all the places you've ever dreamed of going."

Yes, yes, anywhere you want to take me. We'll leave, right this second. Without packing or telling anyone we're going.

I grab Adam's hand. And I run, we run together. He holds on tightly and laughs alongside me. The wind flows through our hair and blood rushes to our cheeks. Our hearts race.

At some point, his hand slips from mine, but I don't care. I can't stop. My lungs burn. My legs are robust. And I'm alive, invincible and energised and vital.

Adam, mid-sentence of a long and convoluted joke, holds the office door open and we run straight into you, Cat, with your screwed-up cat's eyes glinting dangerously as you try to make sense of what you're seeing.

"Oh, hello Adam," you say with a strangled smile. "I brought my lunch back to keep you company, but you'd gone." Your eyes flicker briefly towards me.

"Yes." He sits at his desk and prepares for the afternoon's tasks. I think he winks at me, but I can't be certain.

I'm shocked you can be so easily dismissed. Surely there's a rule, written or otherwise, which says you'll always be first, always best, always get exactly what—and *who*—you want.

You're stunned too, it appears. Your top lip twitches, your eyes widen. But you're Cat, and you don't give up so easily. You take a deep breath and adopt a dazzling smile.

"We're thinking of having a quick drink after work tonight, if you fancy it, Adam?"

"Oh? It's not Friday. I thought you went out on Fridays."

Karen looks up and follows the conversation with a frown and a silent sigh. Manda glances at Karen and rolls her eyes.

"Getting this project off the ground has been full-on; I could do with unwinding a little." You drift between desks, making sure he's watching. "And it's ages until Friday."

"Oh, well, okay. Julia, you'll come, won't you?"

Silence sweeps through the room. Karen and Manda hold their breath, biting back little smirks; you and I exchange taut glances.

"I don't think so," I say, looking down to my keyboard.

"Just this once," Adam persists. His imploring nod is almost imperceptible. "I owe you a drink as a thank-you for all the help you've given me."

"I—er…" *No, no, I'm not supposed to… and yet… how tempting it is.*

"Great." He turns back to you with a satisfied grin. "Sorted."

Five of us leave the office at five o'clock, but only three of us enter the Cherry Tree pub—our customary venue for countless Christmas lunches, leaving dos, and apparently Friday evening drinks. Adam pulls out his wallet and turns to ask us what we want. "Where did Karen and Manda go?"

"They had something else on," you say, slowly, pointedly.

I hide a smirk because I suddenly realise: this was supposed to be a date, just the two of you. Karen and Manda were never invited. You wanted Adam all to yourself. I bet you hate me right now, don't you? More than usual, I mean—and for once, I'm all right with that.

We take our drinks to the table, and you inch your chair as close to Adam's as you're able. I'm opposite; I spot the confused, mock-panic in his eyes.

You drink even quicker than you talk, Cat, did you know that? You barely let your glass settle on the table before taking another sip, and it's soon empty so you totter to the bar for another. Adam and I have barely begun our pints.

"Perhaps I shouldn't have invited you," he says, glancing over at you. "This is weird. Is this weird?"

"Not if you know Cat well. This is pretty standard for her. Would you rather I leave you two alone?"

"Don't even think about it."

You bring a tray to the table—a glass of wine for yourself and three shot glasses. "Shots!" you yell and the other patrons —all seven of them (two with dogs because it's only half-past five in the afternoon)—stare with irritation.

"Not for me, I'm driving," Adam says, and I simply shake my head, so you down all three—shot, shot, shot.

"We'll be going out for Christmas, of course. We go into town afterwards. Dave organises a meal, then leaves us to it. You never normally bother coming out after, do you Julia?"

"Not usually."

"Last year was a riot. We got into this really exclusive club and met up with the IT lads. Actually, I think we gate-crashed a party at the casino—I was their lucky charm, *of course*." You hold your hands up to frame your face.

Adam sips his lager and stacks several beer mats on the edge of the table, preparing to flip them.

"I was wearing the shortest skirt you can imagine. I don't think the bouncer was going to let us in, but he ogled my legs and opened the door straight away. Sometimes you've got to use your talents to get what you want, don't you…?" You turn to me and cast your eyes over my brown knee-length dress and cardigan. "Well, maybe not you, Julia, but you know what I mean…"—you squeeze Adam's hand—"don't you, Adam?"

"Another drink, Julia?" he asks. I want to say no, but he raises his eyebrows, silently pleading with me. "Just a half?"

You look at your glass, still half full, and for a moment I'm sure you'll down it so Adam will offer to buy you another, but you take a sip and put it back down. Your eyes linger on him as he crosses the room.

"I think he fancies me, don't you? After this one, you need to make your excuses so I can have him all to myself."

At the bar, Adam hears every word. He looks alarmed and shakes his head violently. I laugh out loud but manage to turn it into a cough so not to arouse your suspicion.

"This is a pretty nice place—I've not been here before." He puts our drinks on the table and pulls his chair further around the table before he sits. Not to be closer to me, but to be further away from you. I notice it; you must too, right? "Any decent pubs around your way?" he asks me.

"I'm not really sure. I don't—"

"Ha! Julia having a social life, now that's funny. Oh, but: didn't you have a boyfriend once? He came to pick you up. A short guy, I forget his name." You sway a little in your seat and take a gulp of wine. "One boyfriend... bless. I bet all you did was hold his hand." You snort a laugh and reach for Adam's arm.

"There's a band playing here later, if—" Adam says brightly, leaning across the table to act as a shield.

"In fact, there's a strong possibility Julia, poor ickle Julia is still—"

"—you fancy it. We can pop out for fish and chips and—"

"—is *still*"—you raise a finger to your lips—"a virgin. *Ssshh*."

The whole pub is silent at that very moment. I'm sure everyone is laughing and pointing, just like at school. I'm sure a spotlight has been switched on above me.

I stand abruptly. It's too much. "I have to go."

My face is bright red. I flail around, gathering my coat and bag, getting twisted in the strap and drawing further attention.

"I have to go."

"Julia, wait..." Adam disentangles himself from your grasp. I'm already at the door. "I'll give you a lift. Wait a second."

You don't look up. You lean back in your chair, smirking with satisfaction, and swirl wine around the glass. You know you've trounced me, finally and oh so completely, and you didn't even plan it.

I shake my head, my entire life blurring before me, lurching in a wretched and irrevocable trajectory.

"Julia!"

I'm falling into the freezing night air and running away.

I'm a fifteen-year-old girl, pretending to be grown-up, and failing.

A Girl Who Could

In my world, I am fifteen: the age I was when I met Rachel Carr, the age I was when Rachel Carr killed herself with a tonne of painkillers and a bottle of rum. The brown stuff, the stuff which burns your insides as it goes down so you can trace its passage through your body with your finger. The stuff that tastes like it's past the sell-by-date.

I need you to know that, because it impedes every decision I've ever made, every 'no' that should have been a 'yes', every left turn instead of right. I'm vulnerable in a way you've never experienced. I am an eternal child in an adult world.

I imagine how I must appear to you, to Adam, to everyone in that pub. My simplicity and naivety shining like a beacon. I've lived with it for a long time, and I don't want to anymore.

I want to grow up, to be the person I should have become. I want to stand in front of my parents and tell them they had no right to take control of a life which wasn't theirs.

My life. This is *my* life.

But where do I start?

In my world, a world so far from here, I love being me. I'm strong and happy and fun to be with. I'm surrounded by friends, yet like to spend time alone as well—going to the gym, visiting museums and sitting in the café afterwards to think about what I've seen. I'm learning to paint with watercolours and to ice-skate. Maybe I have a boyfriend, maybe I don't. In the summer, a group of us go surfing and light barbeques on the beach as the sun sets. I love living in my sweet little flat, and sometimes inviting my parents over for Sunday lunch. I even enjoy spending Christmas Day with them, knowing I'll be leaving to meet friends before EastEnders comes on.

I don't want anything special. I want what other people have.

But I'm never going to have any of these things unless I change before it's too late.

***

You're watching me from your desk, but your hangover is dulling your arrogance. What happened after I left last night? Did Adam feel sorry for you in your intoxicated state and drive *you* home instead of me? Did you invite him in? He won't look at me, so I'm taking my cues from you. He's quieter than usual, and I think I've ruined everything.

No. You. You've ruined everything for me.

In my world... it would all be so different.

*

64

At lunchtime, I grab my coat and run down the stairs. Out on the street, I briefly wonder how I got here, then head for the newsagent to buy the local Gazette. I sit in the small, gated park opposite, trying to turn the pages with my gloved hands. When I reach the Flats to Let section, I take a calming breath, and run my finger down the brief yet fascinating descriptions —visualising myself in each and every apartment on offer.

It's a whim, a stupid fantasy I allow myself to get caught up in. I've felt like this before, I'm sure I have. The idea will fade soon enough. I'll talk myself out of it, because at the time it made sense, Adam was catching my eye across the office and smiling supportively when you were being ridiculous. He was walking with me along the road and encouraging me to try new things. He was buying me a drink and almost, so very nearly, reaching to brush his finger against mine.

And now, what? He's realised I'm not the person he thought I was, or you lured him away with whispered flirtations in the pub after I left. Or worse. I brace myself for the notion of the two of you together. I'd wanted him to be strong enough to resist you, but maybe no one can, maybe you *do* always get what you want, no matter what.

I glance down and read about a large, sunny room, south-facing, with a kitchenette in the corner, and a good-sized bedroom. I stand at the original French windows which open onto a Juliet balcony. I sit on a white leather sofa, reading novels on a Sunday afternoon. My mother, busily vacuuming and washing and dusting in her dark terraced house, tuts at such slothfulness.

"Mum, I'm leaving home. I've got a place." My bags are by the door. I've been packing for the past week.

"Don't be silly. You're not old enough—you're only fifteen."

"Actually, I'm thirty." I scoop my holdall from the floor. *"My taxi's here. I'll invite you over when I'm settled."*

"You can't go. I won't let you." She stands across the front door, blocking my exit.

"I'll scream if you don't let me past."

No, not that. Too childish.

"It's not your choice, Mum. This is my life."

"You can't go. You need me."

"No, you only think I need you. Guess what, I don't. I found a flat all by myself, and I've paid for it all by myself. You're not going to stop me anymore." I step around her and hurry down the garden path. *"Quick,"* I tell the driver, and he pulls away as Mum runs along the street after me. I haven't even told her my address. I smile and wonder what take-away to get tonight.

I allow myself one last look over the adverts, one last dream, then fold the paper carefully and leave it on the bench as I walk away. Maybe someone else will find their ideal flat among those listings, someone else will sit in front of those French windows, south-facing. I idle back to the office, and sigh as I stand at the foot of the stairs. Steep, insurmountable.

So close, I came so close.

"Everything okay?" Adam asks, before I realise anyone's in the room.

"I thought you'd be at lunch."

"I like eating here. I like the peace." He points to his lunch-box—white Tupperware, like the one Mum leaves out for me. "So?"

"I went for a walk."

"But you're okay?"

"What is this? Yes, I'm fine." I stop. Bite my tongue.

"I'm so sorry about last night."

"It doesn't matter. It's what she does. I should've known better."

"Well, maybe next time—"

You burst into the office, mid-way through a diatribe about a new barista who mistook full-fat milk for the skimmed and completely ruined your pre-Christmas diet. Karen murmurs supportively. Manda manages, "Ah, well," with indifference, as if she's heard it a thousand times. Or perhaps she's also spotted the half-eaten bar of chocolate in your top drawer.

Maybe next time... Adam had started to say. But now he's on the phone and trying to locate an important document, and he'll forget all about *maybe next time.* I stare wistfully into the space above his head and imagine a large sunny room with French windows.

An email pings into my inbox. From Adam. *Meet me outside in 5 mins.* Then he stands and leaves the room without a word.

What's going on? Do I trust him? Should I? I look at each of you at your desks, working away: Dave head down, chewing on the end of his pen; Manda waiting in a queue on the phone while doodling on the back of an envelope; Karen printing copies of a document and organising the pages; you typing and tutting.

Normal stuff. None of you look remotely interested in Adam's departure or my reaction. Is this a set-up, a trap?

I wait almost five minutes, glancing at the clock with rising apprehension. Do I, or don't I?

I almost don't, and then I do. I slip from my seat and pause with my hand on the door, expecting you to look up, expecting a smirk of anticipation to cross your face. You don't. It doesn't. I'm too trusting, that's what Mum says. It's the reason she gives for me still living at home. She says I wouldn't survive in the real world.

Adam's waiting in the corridor and opens the door to the stairwell when I approach.

"What's up?"

"I wanted to finish our conversation."

"Okay." Butterflies and wasps fight in my stomach.

"I was wondering if you were busy tonight. The Christmas market's just opened and I thought we could go. Also," he adds before I've processed the invitation, "I wanted to do this." And he kisses me.

He kisses me.

His lips tremble and there's a shadow of uncertainty across his face, but he recovers quickly and smiles as he draws back.

"What are—?"

"So, you'll come out with me tonight?"

I nod because I don't trust the words. Words work against me; they say things I don't really mean.

He smiles slowly. "Good. You go back in first, it'll look less suspicious. And don't blush."

I don't want to go anywhere; I want to wallow in his kiss. A surge of excitement floods every cell of my body, and I almost skip along the corridor.

In my world, everything happens exactly like this.

***

"Are you okay?" Adam asks. "You're shivering."

"It's cold!" And I'm nervous, scared, exhilarated for whatever might come next. We've trawled the market stalls and tried on silly hats and taken photos and sampled deliciously rich hot chocolate, and Adam's bought small gifts for his sister and mother.

"You should have bought the lion hat. Shall we go back?" He takes my arm and pulls.

"No, it was hideous. And photographic evidence exists—I think that's enough."

"You looked cute."

I look away and so does he. Shyness isn't something I'd associate with Adam, or anyone—to be honest. It's my thing. But here he is, laughing self-consciously.

"How about a drink before we go?"

Go? Surely not; it's too early, too soon. I want this evening to last forever.

"Great."

The pub across the road from the market is busy when we arrive. People congregate on the pavement cigarette in hand, baubles and tinsel dangle in the windows, Christmas music blasts out each time the door opens.

"Too much?" Adam asks and I shake my head. He holds my hand as we walk in, so we don't get separated.

We queue at the bar and then squeeze ourselves into a tiny gap in the corner. Several fancy-dressed people are chaotically dancing to 'Fairytale of New York', bumping into each other, the tables, and us. They sing along with the chorus and cheer whenever someone spills a drink.

We smile when we catch each other's eye but it's too loud to talk. Is that an excuse? Have we run out of things to say? So far, Adam's filled the pauses with random questions about my favourite films and music, or my childhood, and told me silly stories about his own life. Now, he's looking around the room and drinking; and maybe this is how it ends.

"Oh, shit." I point to the door. "Cat's here."

We dodge left behind a pillar, but you've spotted us and dive across the room.

"Adam!" You hug him and reach up to kiss his cheek. You ignore me. "Come and join us. I'm with the IT bunch."

"Actually, I'm happy here, thanks. With Julia."

"Don't be silly, come on." You grab his hand and start to pull him away.

"Cat, really. We're happy here."

"Have you ever been out with the IT lot? They're such a laugh."

"God, Cat, take a hint, won't you," I say under my breath, though apparently not quietly enough. You and Adam both turn to me in surprise. Adam drinks to hide a chuckle and his hand snakes around my waist; you're opened-mouthed and displeased.

"Well, excuse me, Julia. I was only—"

"And we said no." I look directly at you, holding the gaze, hoping the flashing lights from the tree will hide my blushing.

You hover for a second, then turn and walk back to the IT guys.

I'm shaking. I drink my cider quickly because I don't know what else to do. Adam keeps his hand on the base of my spine. I want to admit I've never stood up to you like that before, not in any one of your incarnations. But it wouldn't make sense. I'd have to explain so much more, and I'm not ready to do that. Instead, I lean against Adam's chest and he kisses the top of my head while the DJ plays 'Frosty the Snowman'.

The Woman Who Will

I wake early the day before Christmas Eve, with a shimmer of excitement in my stomach, just like when I was small and laid out mince pies and a glass of milk for Father Christmas. I grin—my entire body quivering—and hug the duvet. It's the last day of work before the holiday, and even though I have to see you first and sit through the Christmas lunch, I'm smiling, because Adam has invited me back to his afterwards. So, when we leave the pub, and go in different directions, I'll be going with him.

I grin in the shower and sing as I select my clothes, putting an extra top for the pub in my bag, and wriggle in the chair while I eat breakfast and listen to the radio. And not even Mum can damper my spirits. It's a good day.

"What's up with you?" Mum asks, pouring another cup of tea from the pot.

"It's Christmas. Isn't everyone happy at Christmas?"

"Mmm."

"Come on, even you must be a bit excited when you hear a Christmas song on the radio or switch on the tree lights in the morning?"

She shrugs. I consider the last time I saw her smile or laugh, and realise it's been too long to recall. But it's not my problem —not today. I scoop the remainder of my muesli from the bowl and down the last drop of tea.

"I won't be home after work. It's the Christmas lunch and some of us are going out afterwards. Don't wait up."

"Wait! What do you—?"

But I'm gone, bouncing down the garden path before she opens the door to give me the third degree. The bus is pulling up to the stop as I turn the corner, so I jump on, sit down, and anticipate the perfect day ahead.

Excitement turns to unease during the short commute. The what-ifs infiltrate my head. The idea Adam might not be as nice as I think he is, that he's somehow still conspiring with you to tempt me into the biggest deception I've ever had to deal with. That you've waited fifteen years for revenge. I pulled through, and you didn't. I lived. Perhaps you never meant to go through with it; perhaps it was all a game for you, a bluff that went wrong.

Or you were so ensnared in a trauma you never admitted to, you couldn't see another way. Your lies and stories may have hinted at the truth, but we were both too young—far too young —to deal with it.

And the most painful part is, I'll never know what I should have done differently.

I'm not smiling. I'm not excited. Adam and my parents and the office Christmas lunch are a million miles away. I soar high above the bus, above the town, above the tiny people below, and wish I could just keep going.

I'm fifteen. Rachel and I are sitting on the floor of her bedroom; she's reaching for the bottle of rum and unscrewing the lid. I wish I could take it from her and tell her this is not the answer.

My mood doesn't tally with the party atmosphere in the office. But then, it rarely has done before, so it's nothing new. It's disappointing, that's all, after the day started so well. Jollity and optimism are something other people have; I shouldn't have expected it to last.

You're wearing a Christmas jumper as a dress, and it's far too short—especially when you're sitting on the edge of Adam's desk and trying to attract his attention. Between you and me, Cat, I think he's noticed.

He smiles at me—a fusion of 'Hello gorgeous' and 'Help me'. Possibly. I'm fearful my intuition isn't as sharp as I assumed and I'm getting it all wrong. Could I misconstrue a romantic date at a Christmas market and long goodnight kiss? Oh yes, I think I probably could.

"Okay, guys," Dave calls across the room. "I'm not expecting much work from you today, but try to focus for a little while, yes? We'll stop at twelve. I've booked our usual table at the Cherry Tree."

"Don't know why we can't just go home early," you grumble. "Don't know why we're forced to spend *lunch* together." You glare at me. I'm the one you don't want to be forced to sit next to. This cheers me a little, to be honest.

"Because it's the season of goodwill to all," Dave replies. "My goodwill for paying, and your goodwill for spending quality time with your esteemed colleagues."

"Uh. Whatever." You flounce back to your own desk like a six-year-old at someone else's birthday party. "You'll be coming out for a few drinks afterwards, won't you Adam? We always make a night of it."

"Who's going?" he asks casually, knowing the answer.

You mutter a reply about Manda and Karen, and meeting up with the IT guys but not the blokes from Marketing who are abnormally boring. "And anyone else who tags along, I guess." Again, you look at me with a withering expression.

The morning passes quickly. A flurry of last-minute issues to sort out means none of us notices the time, so it's a surprise when Dave announces: "Pens down, troops. The pub beckons."

Previously, these annual get-togethers meant burrowing into a corner, eating as quickly as possible, and spending an inordinate length of time in the loos. Today—despite the resurgence of my scepticism of Adam—I'm curious to observe how you'll act around him. And, indeed, how he'll respond. I've been silent this morning, unable to meet his eye, even when he offered me coffee and I declined. He might have already decided I'm too much effort.

I sit between Dave and Adam. Adam saved the seat for me and prevented you sitting down when you tried (I wanted to applaud). You shoved Manda out of the way to sit opposite, though, stretching your legs under the table to *accidentally* find his. You've kicked me twice already.

The purr of conversation flows over me, but I don't seem to fit into either of them; I'm tucked into a fissure between both. Dave, Manda, and Karen are discussing last night's cheesy Christmas film on Channel 4, and you're trying to wheedle out of Adam if he has a *special someone* to cuddle up with on Christmas morning. And you're not giving up, are you, Cat?

I drink my wine and feel foolish for letting myself think this year might be any different. Except, I guess, with Adam next to me, it is. Isn't it?

Adam, who seems to be transforming me slowly into something new, through the sheer chance of meeting him one damp day in the middle of November. Adam, who I hope sees through your schemes and spite. Adam who, while politely eschewing your advances and trying to change the subject, is reaching for my hand under the table and running his thumb across my palm, sending shivers along my spine.

"So, what did you ask Father Christmas for this year, Julia?" He takes advantage of the bar staff bringing out the food to turn away from you while you're distracted.

"Oh, he doesn't really take notice of me anymore."

"Too good or too naughty?"

I blush.

"Julia's always good. The goodest of us all." You giggle, but no one joins in.

"Perhaps you need to do something to get his attention?" His voice is deep, *sexy* even, almost a whisper. He raises an eyebrow and turns to his meal. Earlier doubts are dispersing —can it be that easy to know he's genuine, or am I simply too gullible? I wish I understood.

"I'm sure mummy and daddy fill your stocking. You *do* still live at home with them, don't you?"

I take a breath and smile widely at you. "Why yes, of course they do, silly me. If I don't get a Princess Barbie this year, I'm going to be ever so sad."

You look confused—as though you know I'm joking, but I may not be; I probably am, but you're unsure whether to laugh or not. Laughing at me: good. Laughing at my jokes: bad.

The meal takes precedence after a while and the only conversation is about the food on our plates and if anyone wants another drink. Once we're finished, Dave coughs to gain our attention and makes his usual speech about how well we've worked this year, how our targets have been met, and how important the team is. I always chuckle at that part—*team* is a tenuous word for our office. Then, he shakes hands with each of us, wishes us Merry Christmas, and leaves.

It's awkward, now, the five of us.

Karen and Manda are chatting between themselves. You're leaning on the table, arms crossed to make your cleavage that little bit extra, talking about nightclubs and *after* nightclubs and how Christmas lets you do all kinds of secret things.

Adam's sitting back in his chair, trying to be as far away from you as possible, focused on his pint. You don't let it stop you; you talk a little louder, pout, giggle. You try every trick you know. Sorry, Cat, but he's holding my hand under the table again, our fingers laced together. I thought you'd like to know that.

"So, you'll be heading off as well, Julia, right? Won't it be past your bedtime soon?" you snigger.

I pretend to consider. "No, I don't think I will yet."

"Oh, but…" Your smile flickers briefly. "It's just you usually leave about now. You don't really… stay… do you?" You smile brightly and insincerely.

"No, not usually. But I think I will today. In fact, I'm going to get another drink." I drain my glass and stand. "Does anyone else want anything? Cat, can I buy you a drink?"

We spend another hour in the pub. Karen and Manda leave to go to a house party—they were trying to entice you along with them, but there was no way you planned to go anywhere without Adam. I know you—you think all you need to do is bat your eyes and purr seductively to get your man. Not this time, though. He's not being rude, he's not ignoring you or anything, but he's not initiating conversation either. He's talking to me, and tolerating you butting in. He's leaning towards me, closer and closer, and you're oblivious.

Once our glasses are empty, your eyes shine. This is it—I'll go my way, and you and Adam will be tipsy and at a loose end... won't you?

"Well, Merry Christmas, Cat. We're going to make a move."

You frown, trying to work out what's happening. While we wrap up in coats and gloves, you're *still* clutching onto some kind of hope. When Adam takes my hand as we walk away, I think that's when the penny drops. I glance back and you're standing there with your arms held out, as if to say, "what the hell...?"

"Back to mine, then?"

I nod silently while he flags down a taxi. In the back seat, we're silent. The world whooshes past. Adam lives between the city centre and the suburbs, where Georgian town houses have been converted to flats and there are small pockets of land where kids are playing football. Normal things are happening all around me, but this journey, this moment, isn't normal. It only takes five minutes. We're here and I'm not ready.

Adam's flat doesn't have a real fire like it did in my dream. Oh, if only this was a dream and I could be that confident. But it's not—outside it's almost dark, dull, real.

There are shelves lining the walls stuffed with books, along with a couple of photos in frames. A guitar leans against the sofa. Adam ushers me further into the room, and we stand awkwardly face-to-face.

"You play?" I indicate the guitar.

"A little." He laughs nervously. I fiddle with the zip of my jacket. "God, what am I thinking? Here, let me have your coat." I hand it to him, and he pauses indecisively before chucking it onto a chair. He turns back to me and seems at a loss. "Um, coffee? Wine?"

"Wine would be lovely."

I lean against the door frame of the small kitchen to watch him. His hand shakes as he pours and the wine splashes onto the counter. He hands me a glass, his fingers brushing mine as I take it from him.

"You're really here. I didn't think..." He chuckles. "I might have thought about this a couple of times."

"Oh."

He brushes hair from my face and his cold index finger traces the line of my jaw and down my neck. He steps closer—tall and overwhelming—and kisses me so gently I sigh.

"You're shivering."

"I guess I'm nervous."

"You don't need to be."

"You don't know anything about me."

"What would you like me to know?"

I could say anything. I could lie, reinvent myself, create a new persona. Be whoever I want. I've spent so long concealing who I am, erecting barriers, walking away when anything got too candid, because it was safer. But there are different kinds of *safe*—those where you don't allow any chance of risk or potential happiness, and those where the people in your life stand alongside you, no matter what. Maybe I've clung to the wrong path. It's hard to envisage what the truth will be, but I don't want to lie anymore.

Adam's eyes are penetrating and patient, and right now, the past doesn't matter.

"Nothing," I say, and I reach up and kiss him and we topple onto the sofa.

***

Mum's at the kitchen table when I get home the next morning, a mug of tea in front of her, arms folded. She's been waiting for me. I wonder how long she'd have sat there if, say, I'd gone shopping on my way back or stayed with Adam for another night. He'd tried to get me to stay—holding me firm in his bed, legs and arms wrapped around me—pouting as I withdrew and hunted for my clothes.

Mum's folded arms hold a language of their own. Upset, miffed, cold, irritated, frustrated, satisfied: each one implicit instantly in any situation. Right now, her arms—her fingers tapping against the mug—are verging on furious. I hesitate. I'm a fifteen-year-old girl coming back down to Earth with a thud. I stand tall, pretending nothing is amiss, and cross the kitchen to put the kettle on.

"Where've you been?"

"I told you I was staying out."

"I didn't know where you were, who you were with…"

"I texted you."

"Anything could have happened."

"I was with the people from work. I told you."

"Was that boy there?"

Boy! She thinks my friends are all fifteen too. "Boy?"

"Don't play innocent with me. Adam. Is that where you've been *all* night? With him?"

"And what if it was?" I spin around with a flash of anger. "I said I wouldn't be home. I'm not a child anymore. I'm a grown woman. I could stay out every single night if I wanted to. In fact, I could *move* out."

I flinch at my own words. *Move out?* That was unexpected. I maintain eye-contact, bracing myself for the impending fight.

Mum's gaze bores into me. I despise her weaponised silences; they seem so contrived. She finishes her tea, stands, carefully pushes the chair under the table, and leaves the room.

I'm thirty. I'm an adult. I am strong and capable. I'm thirty, an adult; strong and capable...

But the words are corroding as I say them.

Cruel and Malicious Creatures

What cruel and malicious creatures my parents must have been to lock me away from the world, to hide me from the adventure and freedom of growing up, from the slip-ups I would have no doubt made and the lessons I'd have learned, from the pain and joy and confusion.

How strange it must have appeared to people on the outside, a girl of sixteen, seventeen, eighteen being escorted around town by the hand; being dropped off at school and picked up again every afternoon; never permitted to go shopping with friends on Saturday afternoon or to the cinema or around to their house. How strange for that girl to not actually have mates to do those things with, but to be shadowed by hushed silences and distrust wherever she went. How strange for her to require, to depend on, that cocoon of parental fortification to soothe her and make the world outside disappear.

That girl... me.

And yet, I can't relate to her. I don't remember those things as personal memories. I share her story. I smile sadly at her, wishing I'd done something to help. I glare at her parents, so cruel and malicious, creating a prison this girl didn't deserve. They would say they were protecting her, keeping her from the harm she was so capable of inflicting on herself, of allowing others to inflict upon her. With hindsight, I say they acted with selfishness, wanting to keep her ever closer so they'd never again risk experiencing the panic and fear they felt the day the police arrived to tell them she was in hospital.

For the months, years that followed, my mother's vigilance didn't seem improper or overpowering. I knew it wasn't how other people, other girls, other women lived their lives, but it never felt truly wrong until the day, the very moment, I met Adam.

Suddenly I saw myself through his eyes—his being the only ones which have ever mattered.

I am not the person I envisaged becoming when I was fifteen, in those months before Rachel Carr walked into my maths class. I wanted to travel, to spend summers working in bars on the east coast of Australia, and perhaps remain there, meet the man of my dreams, have kids with Australian accents.

Admittedly, they were plans I'd heard other people mention, ideas I'd latched on to because they seemed typical. But they were just fantasies, added to my world of them, to diffuse the torments and bullying; keeping alive the notion there was something afterwards, something better than this. Like I'd told Rachel.

Maybe, even at fifteen, I wasn't the person I ought to have been. Perhaps I've taken side-steps throughout my life and now I'm so far off course I'll never really know who I am.

My parents were in the room when I woke up, faces haggard and tear-stained, outlines of themselves. They squeezed my hand, and leant over the bed to hug me, one on each side. So terrified. So elated I'd opened my eyes, finally. They cried and called for the nurse. And I was swept into a frenzy of activity.

There was a window beside me. The sky was stormy and black, and branches of exposed trees swayed violently. A bird struggled to fly in a straight line; clouds swooshed past. I wasn't at home—there were no trees outside my bedroom window at home. And I wasn't dead.

Not dead, but groggy and thirsty; my throat sore from where they'd pumped my stomach. My dreams had been chaotic, abstract. I'd felt dazed and dizzy, as if riding an infinite rollercoaster. Now I was awake, the dizziness intensified. Memories flitted about, but they made no sense. As I tried to grab them and tie them down, they vanished.

Why am I here instead of at Rachel's? Why were we at *Rachel's* instead of school? And where is she? Where's Rachel?

"Have some water, love. Lie down, try not to get excited."

At various intervals, one or other of my parents would sob with joy or smother me with embraces, or simply stare with a lopsided, resolute smile. I was swimming in a void. I'd moved beyond feeling anything, set it aside, so convinced that I was dead and no longer in want of such burdens. I pretended to be relieved and happy. I offered tears and hugs of my own, smiles when they arrived, *I love yous* when they left. But really, there was nothing inside me anymore.

For days, no one spoke about what had happened. I was forced to generate my own version of events, which might still be wildly different from the truth.

I'd sat nervously on Rachel's bedroom floor, waiting for her to tell me what to do. Two bottles of rum and several blister packs of tablets on the carpet in front of us. That's all I recalled. My parents provided ambiguous, poker-faced responses to my questions. At least, Mum did. Dad slowly drew back, sitting a little further away each day. He could barely look at me.

They made no mention of Rachel, although I asked, or what we'd done. Even the nurses seemed to whisper the word, tried to deny it. Through listening carefully to their conversations as I plodded to and from the toilet, through piecing together the snippets and judgemental glances, I knew Rachel was dead long before they told me. I was fifteen-years-old, too young to deal with any of this. My body ached and my heart wept.

***

Christmas in a house full of adults is a non-event—or perhaps just in this house where my every glass of wine is monitored and Christmas cracker jokes remain unread. Once I turned eighteen, gift-giving diminished to an envelope with money in it, and decorations were pared down to a tree and some tinsel draped over picture frames.

After lunch—turkey carved at one o'clock on the dot—Mum potters until it's time for the Queen's speech, Dad snoozes and pretends he isn't, and I go to my room. It becomes a normal day.

Usually. This year, once the dishes are done, I grab my coat, no longer able to abide the frostiness and tedium.

"Are you meeting *him*?" Mum calls sharply and I leave without answering.

No, I'm not, actually. Adam's with his family in Nottingham today. He won't be back until the day after tomorrow. But she doesn't need to know—let her think what she wants, it's no longer my concern.

The streets are bright and frosty. Lights twinkle from the houses and kids are playing on new bikes and skateboards. I stroll without a destination, greeting others who are walking too with a smile and a *Merry Christmas*. People are wandering along with dogs that linger to inspect every blade of grass and gatepost; or they're striding with purpose and large bags of gift-wrapped boxes; or surging in cheerful flocks consisting of children and parents and grandparents.

I'm the only person totally alone, but it's okay. It really is. I text Adam—the third time today—but as with the previous ones, he doesn't reply.

Busy with his family, I tell myself, staring at the screen for a moment, then tucking my phone in my pocket.

"Or scared off," says Gavin with contempt.

Gavin? Oh no, not him. I'm not ready to face him.

"You haven't changed, then. Still clingy and pitiful."

"I wasn't either of those things!"

He shrugs. He matches my pace as I speed up to avoid him. "Do you love him?"

"I've only known him a few weeks, it's too early for that."

"You said you loved me after three days."

"Did I? I don't remember."

"Although you didn't, not really. It's something you tried to convince yourself. I could tell when you looked at me."

"And yet, you asked me to marry you."

"I know. I was young and foolish. And God, I was such a nerd."

"I did. I did love you."

"You were trying to escape."

"No." I didn't realise there was anything to escape from back then. We were both lost, neither of us fitted into the norm; always overlooked.

"Is that what you're doing now? Do you still need someone to run to? Aren't you old enough to stand on your own two feet?"

I pause. I frown. I don't know.

"Where are you? Are you happy?"

But he's gone and I'm alone.

The wind is icy when I turn the next corner and my face tingles. My fingers, despite my gloves, are becoming numb. Yet, going home is not an attractive prospect, so I march towards the pub two streets over. Blaring music and the roar of voices hits me when I open the door and hesitate. So many strangers who'll look up and eye me with ridicule. Last time I was in a busy pub, Adam was there to dilute my anxiety. Before I can walk away, a couple appear behind me and nudge me inside.

No one looks. No one cares I'm alone. I feel myself unfurling, standing a little taller. A bloke in an elf costume wishes me, "Merry Christmas, love," and tells me to get a drink inside me. So, I do.

I sip cider and watch other people enjoying themselves, and being on the periphery feels okay. A different bloke, and then a woman, both try to include me in the dancing; I smile and shake my head, holding up my drink as an excuse. Once, I'd have been torn apart with envy—all these people sharing a moment I was excluded from. Perhaps I was *never* excluded, perhaps people were always trying to involve me, but my own diffidence prevented me from noticing.

Adam texts: Merry Xmas. It's hectic here. Two babies and a toddler all want to use me as a trampoline.

Me: I'm in a pub!

Adam: Who with? Should I be jealous?

Me: No one. On my own.

Adam: Good for you. You okay?

Me: Yeah, I think so.

Adam: Gotta go. See you very soon xx

Two kisses! I look at them for a while, resisting the temptation to analyse them.

I finish my pint and edge towards the exit. The bloke in the elf costume dances alongside me to the door and bows as I leave. I am thirty. I'm an adult. I am strong, and I can drink alone in a pub and be comfortable with it. I am capable.

***

"Happy New Year," Adam whispers at the stroke of midnight. All around us, people are hugging and kissing and raising their glasses. We sing 'Auld Lang Syne' and I don't want the night to end. This is perfect.

I am strong. I am capable. It's a new year, a new beginning. My year. My beginning.

I nuzzle into Adam's torso and reach up to kiss him, holding his face between my hands, inhaling the scent of his aftershave, the heat of his body against mine. I smile with contentment, and Adam is curious because he doesn't yet understand.

We walk home so late it's early. A few people are idling along in various states of intoxication and merriment. Adam is drunk and sleepy, leaning against me to stop himself stumbling. I'm lucid and enthused by the possibilities of a new me.

"What's your New Year's Resolution?" he asked earlier.

"I don't make them."

"Why not?" He was almost aghast, as if it was an essential path into the next year.

"Because they never last—you break them after a couple of days and feel bad about yourself."

Now, though, curling up in bed while he's faintly snoring beside me, ideas are emerging. Not ideas, really, snippets of daydreams, vague musings, cusp-of-dawn fantasies that catch me by surprise. I close my eyes and a new world is in front of me.

Tomorrow

In my world, sometimes, Rachel isn't dead at all. I'm in ignorance of this, of course. In this world, my parents orchestrated many lies over the course of my stay in hospital, forcing others to comply with their increasing mesh of fictions to control every part of my life, to keep the secret. Every year, I visit a cemetery where she was never buried, blaming her for the myriad of imperfections I've acquired.

In this world, one day, I am walking along the road, a long way from home, and she's in front of me suddenly. Grown up and wearing a smart work outfit, with her hair pulled into a neat ponytail. It appears, from her look of shock and surprise, she believed the same about me—that I was dead.

I reach out first, touching her shoulder and prodding without a word, to make certain it's really her. For a second, I want to hug her and shriek with joy and ask her what happened back then, ask her why no one told us we were alive.

But no. I can't. This is *her* fault. This pathetic waste of a life is her fault. I slap her face, hard, producing a lurid red handprint on her cheek. She slaps me back. We stare at each other, hatred filling every inch of our bodies and souls, the pain stinging. And she walks away, brushing past me without a word, without a glance.

***

"Mum, Dad, I'm moving out."

Outside, it's grey and dreary, rain starting to patter against the window, so I know this isn't a dream. The wood burner is crackling in the corner, but I'm cold, wrapped in an oversized cardigan. It's almost the end of January; dawn and dusk are starting to stretch themselves out, but spring is a long way off.

Mum chuckles. Dad shakes his head. They both turn away.

"I said, I'm moving out."

"You're a dreamer, Julia," Mum says, dismissing this bold, brave statement of mine. She's ironing—smoothing out each item until it achieves a higher level of perfection, spraying and respraying as tiny crinkles appear. She turns her back on me to fold a t-shirt.

I am expected to leave, dismissed like a child to go to my room and think about what I've said. Discussion over.

"No."

They look up. I can't remember the last time I said *no* to them.

With their gaze on me, my resolve stumbles. I close my eyes and recall my rehearsed speech. "I'm thirty. I've got a good job, and I want—need—my own home."

Mum sets the iron down on the board and brushes the back of her hand across her eyes. She wants me to think she's distressed, crying even, but it's an act she uses in almost any situation where she hasn't automatically won. I turn to Dad, who is looking at Mum not me, and I feel I'm hurting him more.

"I love you both. You know that. I appreciate everything you've done for me. I know it's been difficult." *I'm not the person I should be, because of you. You're smothering me.* "But it's time I—"

"Moved away, rejected us, abandoned us?" suggests Mum, arms folded, glare unwavering.

"—grew up and let you have your lives back. I can't be a child forever. I'm positive you didn't expect me to still be living here in my thirties."

"I don't see why not. It's cheaper than paying rent, for a start. You've got company whenever you want it. You get meals cooked and your washing done." She gestures to the clothes basket and pile of ironing inside.

"Dad?"

He says nothing, like usual. He purses his lips as if preventing the words from escaping. Words of censure? Of support? I wish I knew. The silence looms around us.

"I'm not asking. I'm telling you this is going to happen soon. I'm letting you know."

"You ungrateful cow!" Mum shrieks. Both Dad and I recoil. "After all we've done for you, to keep you safe, to keep you from... from harm."

"Bev…" Dad shakes his head slowly.

Mum closes her eyes and covers her mouth with her hand.

I don't understand, and then I do.

"You thought I was going to try again? You thought I was going to…?"

I sit heavily, stunned. Gazing in horror. All this time, *this* is what they were thinking. Dad sits forward, glancing between the two of us.

"Julia, I…"

"No…"

I see Rachel laughing in front of me as she pours too much rum into her mouth and it spills down her chin, dark and sticky. I laugh too, trying to sit up straight and prevent the world from spinning, because what a joke this is, what a prank. So dizzy, so tired. Unable to keep our eyes open.

One more drink, one more tablet.

At some point, we stopped laughing. I can't remember when.

"No. That's not what… I wasn't. I was never going to…"

I can't catch my breath. My throat tightens. My head spins. I fumble for the arm of the sofa to stop myself falling, tumbling.

Everything is an illusion.

I can grab my surroundings with both hands, pull it apart and push it back together, feel rain on my face and rough sand beneath my fingers and toes. I can make believe.

Yet, the life I thought I was leading is different to how others see it—even my own parents. Have I *ever* been in the real world?

I withdraw, one anguished step at a time, removing myself from this room, this house, this life.

My mother is steadfast with the satisfaction she saved me from myself, the belief she was right. I want to yell at them; to experience a rage unrestrained, to see the horror and confusion on their faces. But I'm always controlled, always quiet and reflective, watching never acting.

I fight against self-imposed chains, and they pull tighter and tighter.

We eat dinner together, barely an hour later, in silence. We spend the evening in separate rooms. The next day, and the next. All silent.

I circle adverts in the local papers and peruse estate agent windows. I find a few flats which appear suitable, and Adam comes with me to view them, offering opinion when required, making suggestions when asked. We sit in a coffee shop afterwards, discussing the merits and drawbacks. I sign the contract and pay my deposit. I move out within the month.

We are silent.

***

My flat is peaceful. I stand in the middle of the room and close my eyes. It's not a dream.

Outside, cars drive too fast along residential streets, kids talk loudly as they walk below my window to school, the odd skateboard rolls past, a radio is a muffled murmur from the flat above.

My flat is perfect.

I wear shoes in every room.

I don't unpack my bags straight away.

I cook pasta and don't wash up afterwards.

I watch something other than endless soap operas.

Or I don't put the TV on at all. I read books and listen to music instead. Or revel in the silence.

I eat toast and jam in bed, snuggling down into the duvet, dropping crumbs.

I lock the door and close the curtains. And suddenly, it's real.

"What have you done?" you ask, holding my hand and standing beside me as we stare at the wall. I want to hang a picture, but I'm not sure where.

You look smaller than usual. I am making you smaller.

"I've grown up."

"If that's what you think."

I wait for you to elaborate, casting a glance sideways. You drop my hand and wander across to the shelves, browsing the books, picking up an ornament or two with a sneer. You check the top of the TV for dust, like Mum would do.

"After everything they did for you, this is how you treat them?"

"This is how it's supposed to be. They did too much. They didn't know when to stop. They were suffocating me. It was like dying all over again."

"You haven't died once, yet."

"I almost did."

"Yeah, then you bottled it, didn't you?"

"Get out. This is my flat, and I want you to get out of it."

You consider me carefully. Then smile with a conceding nod. "Of course. But I'll see you soon."

Adam arrives with a bottle of Champagne. He picks me up and twirls me around. "Happy?"

I nod.

He pops the cork and the contents spill over his hand while I try to find some glasses. I only have mugs, hastily grabbed from the cupboard as I was packing, so we drink from them instead. Mine says World's Best Daughter and Adam's is the shape of a chocolate egg.

"To Julia. And to Julia's flat—the very best of flats."

"I can't believe I did it."

"Have you talked to your parents yet?"

I sigh. "I tried. Mum hung up on me. Maybe next week. But now"—I grab his hand and drag him across the room—"come and look. My cooker!"

"Lovely. Can you cook?"

"That's not the point. My fridge!" I open it. Chocolate and wine, mostly. An egg. Half a cucumber.

"Interesting. Glad I brought takeaway."

Into the bathroom. "Look!"

Into the bedroom. He pulls me towards him.

"I like this room the best," he says.

"Why?"

In reply, he lowers me onto the bed and lies beside me, kissing me while the bubbles from the Champagne fizz in my head.

Adam is asleep. It's much later, just before five—dark and silent outside, my clock ticking. His mouth holds a slight smile, his eyelids flicker, betraying the fact he's dreaming. I hope it's a good one, a dream about me maybe. I move closer to rest my head on the pillow beside his, pressing my body against his back. He's warm, his skin musky. I want to kiss him, but I don't want to wake him. I remain as still as possible and imagine.

A small tear slides down my cheek. I have no idea why I'm

crying. Joy, fear excitement, grief? All good reasons, but I don't feel any of them; or I feel them all and it's too much to process. Mostly, I'm confused. This is so right, so perfect. This is how all women my age spend Friday nights—in bed with boyfriends and husbands, planning the weekend, the months, the years. I'm not used to it. When Adam wakes, he'll ask me what I want to do today. We'll go shopping, or to the cinema, or drive to the sea and stop somewhere quaint for lunch. Normal things that normal people do.

"But you're not normal, are you, Julia? You shouldn't be here, with Adam or anyone else. You should be with me, the way we planned it."

"It was your plan, not mine."

"I've been waiting for you. You should've come with me like I asked you to. You left me."

"I'm sorry."

"You were weak."

"No, you wanted me to think *that. You were as bad as everyone else. I let you control me because I didn't know any better. It's different now. I'm different."*

"You sat on my bedroom floor. You chose it. You could have left. You took the pills and drank the rum."

"I didn't want to die. You dragged me along because you were scared. And I thought you weren't scared of anything."

"Scared? Pah! You're the one who spent her life in shadows, too timid to look up."

You vanish before I can reply.

***

I count the weeks we've been together, Adam and I: nine. It seems longer, the way in films people say, *it's like I've known you all my life.* I never used to understand what they meant. We haven't told anyone in work, but Adam thinks Dave knows. He eyes us suspiciously when Adam comes back from lunch a minute or two after me, or makes me a coffee without asking. Little things. Things we should have considered.

"But why shouldn't people know? Wouldn't you like to see their faces when we tell them?"

"Because it's a small office and there are probably company rules against it. Perhaps you could transfer to Accounts—Cat speaks highly of them." I nudge him in the ribs so he knows I'm teasing.

I think you know too, Cat. You scrutinise our every move, our every smile and gesture. You listen to our low-voiced exchanges and make subtle remarks. You're waiting, aren't you? Waiting to pounce, ready to sharpen your claws and steal your prey.

You're talking to Adam when I walk into the office. He stayed at my place last night—mine! I can still hardly believe it—and drove me to work. He parked one street over and we walked in separately.

You're perched on the edge of my desk, with your legs crossed and swinging, and your skirt riding up your thigh. Trying so hard to get Adam to notice you. So hard and so absurd. You're becoming a parody of yourself, which is fascinating to watch in some ways, and uncomfortable in others.

You've lost, Cat. You've lost Adam, and you've finally lost control over me. How does it make you feel? How do you feel, right now?

"It was such a good night, it's a shame you missed it. In fact, it's been ages since you've been out with us—what *have* you been doing with yourself? Come to the gig this weekend!"

You're talking to Adam but looking at me, making clear I am *not* invited.

"I think I'm busy, but... er, thanks."

"My cousin's in this really cool band. We'll get VIP access. You have to come."

His phone rings saving him from responding. You pout and sigh but remain on the edge of my desk.

"Do you mind?" I mime pushing you off and you scowl. Adam smirks.

"Go on," I nudge you, "between you and me... do you really like Adam or are you just trying to make sure I don't have him?"

"No, I really like him." Your face folds into laughter. "Oh, okay. He's all right, I suppose, nothing special though, is he? I can see why you'd be interested. He should *like me more than he likes you. Everyone does because I'm beautiful and perfect."*

"Well, actually, lots of people think you're loud and brash and very obvious. Quite frankly, you're coming across as desperate. Dave's noticed, and the guys from IT. Ask Karen and Manda— they're embarrassed for you."

"They are not! I'm fun and playful. Adam gets it. I think he's starting to turn."

We both look across to Adam who's totally unaware of our out-of-body conversation. He's frozen in time, suspended in my reality.

How could you not fancy Adam, though? It can't all be for my benefit. His eyes are darkly mysterious and brooding, flashing with humour and kindness. His hair is short and messy—without gel, it flops over his forehead. His lips pout when I'm near him, as though they have a mind of their own and can think only of kissing me. His arms are muscular, rippling through his shirt sleeves, and sometimes all I want is to be lifted high into the air and whisked away from this place.

Gavin, in a previous dream, asked if I loved Adam, and I said it was far too early. Now, I think maybe I do. Right now, here in the office, I want to tell him.

All the Days After

Adam talks about the future as though it's guaranteed. Holidays, houses, jobs, moving away. A different town, a different county. He talks about kids. There's so much future in his head.

The more he talks, the bigger the lump in my throat grows, the more the cluster of uneasiness in my stomach distracts me. Not because I doubt I'm in this future, but because I'm certain I am.

He starts so many conversations with, "Have you ever…?"

And my answer is mostly, "No."

It doesn't stop him asking. With every *no* I'm a little less secure, a little more inadequate.

"It doesn't matter," he says, his eyes flashing with passion.

"We'll go to Argentina and Morocco and Croatia"—snatching countries from thin air. I don't even own a passport. "We'll go to Norway to see the Northern Lights, and drink Champagne at the top of the Eiffel Tower."

"You've been to all those places?"

"Not all of them. I'll take you to my favourites and we'll explore new ones together. We'll get lost in strange cities and find bars only the locals know about. I want to change your life, Julia."

"You want to change me?"

"No! No." His face falls, horrified. "That's not what I meant at all. I... I love you for exactly who you are. Travelling won't change you, it'll make... it gives you new experiences." He takes my hand in his. "I wouldn't want to change you," he says in a deep, serious voice. "I love you."

It's the first time he's said that. I know I should reply in kind. But I can't say it. Why not? I've known for a while, yet the words are wedged in my choked-up throat. Instead, I hold his face between my hands, and I kiss him so softly, so gently, so completely, we're both slightly dazed when we pull away.

When Adam leaves, I wait at my window until he appears at the front door, three flights down. I keep the light off, so he won't know I'm here.

He strides along the road to his car—his strong, broad shoulders hunched against the downpour, his hands wedged into his jacket pockets. I watch as if it's the first time I've seen him, like that first day in the office. Indeed, sometimes he's still that stranger to me, someone I've created in a fantasy. I can't reconcile the man who was here only minutes ago with the shape walking away from me.

I watch him drive away as though it's the last time. And I know it isn't, but I'm hollow and mournful. In my bedroom, the unmade bed holds the warmth of our bodies, the indentations of our heads on the pillows. I climb in and curl up on Adam's side. His pillow smells of him, the slightly sweet smell of sex and the beads of sweat which form on his forehead.

Is this you, Cat? Are you doing this to me, making me anxious and fearful? Can't you leave me alone, even now Adam is beside me to ward you off? I should be stronger than this.

It was different tonight, more ardent. We sank into each other, deep and complete. I had the full weight of his body on mine, pressing down. I could feel his breath on my shoulder, his teeth biting softly into me. We lay for a long time, not talking, just listening to the wind whistling around outside. Every so often, Adam squeezed me tightly towards him and buried his face in my hair or kissed the top of my head.

Yet, despite how often he's stayed in the past few weeks, tonight, he got up and dressed and left. I don't know why. What changed? Did I do something wrong? No, forget that—I don't want to know.

Life was easier before Adam. I didn't like it—I hated it—but I'd settled into place and my expectations were low. A couple of months ago, perhaps only weeks, I'd have accepted this shift, this abandonment; I'd have anticipated it. Here one minute, running away the next. No, he didn't run, he wasn't escaping. He kissed me and said, "No, not tonight," when I asked if he wanted to watch a film. "I have to go. I'll see you in the morning."

The sun beats down on me. I lie back on the warm, white sand, and spread my arms and legs out to make a star shape. It's early in the morning; the beach has yet to be overcome with hordes of people intent on ruining my solitude. I don't move. I try to sink into the sand, wriggling slightly so my torso and bottom furrow out a small ditch. Drowning in sand. Is that possible? I don't want to drown; I simply want it to surround me and keep me hidden. There's no one here, and still, I want to hide.

How stupid I am, in both my dreams and my nightmares, that I cannot be the real me. Or maybe, I don't know who the real me is. On an empty beach, with nothing around to anchor me, I cease to exist.

People invade from either side, from the sand dunes behind me, from the lapping surf ahead. My perfect beach is desecrated. I stand and wave, craving just one person to acknowledge me, to turn and notice everything I've so carefully set up has been spoilt, because of all these strangers pouring down on me.

I'm shrinking, smaller and smaller. My waving is pointless. A throng of torsos, of thighs, of knees around me. Smaller and smaller, until.

With no one to notice me, I cease to exist.

***

After weeks of theatre trips and comedy clubs and indoor golf and wrapped-up-in-woolly-jumper picnics, we slow down. We need to find our feet within the relationship, to test if we can sustain it without all the distraction.

In the Kings Arms, my new local, we share cheesy chips and listen to an acoustic duo playing Def Leppard. I dance to the bar, and he watches with a soft smile playing on his lips. And I'm safe and loved.

When we leave, we'll go to my flat, and toast bagels, and eat them in bed, getting crumbs in awkward places.

At first, it was something I'd recall with amazement. Sitting at my desk, the next morning, harbouring our exquisite secret, hardly believing the man across the room, discussing a client's problem with Dave and looking so professional, was the same man who'd stood bare-chested in my kitchen making toast only hours before. And no one knew, not even you, Cat.

I wanted to tell everyone we were almost late because we had sex in the shower, and his wistful smile is because he's thinking about my naked body.

At first. But what about now? I don't know.

Adam is everything I've dreamed of, the person I've waited for.

He makes me laugh; he makes me brave. He shows me I can, rather than caution me I can't. I'm the best version of me, and I'm magnificent. He's edging you out, Cat—your voice is diminishing. I can barely hear you over the tumult of my life bursting wide open.

He protects me, holds me close when we pass rowdy groups in the street, and walks into pubs first and stands slightly in front of me, shielding me until he's had time to access the risks. And yet...

Oh no, not those words, not *that* feeling. Just when everything is so good.

And yet...

Doubt crawls across me. Not a lightning bolt of clarity but snatched moments when I don't feel myself.

I observe the shape of us as if watching two strangers strolling across a park. Two people who are friends, who hold hands and kiss, who are both a little unsure. Tentative, restrained, a space between them—a wall, a barrier so securely assembled we might never be able to break it down: my past.

When Adam is asleep, I tell him everything while he dreams of other things. I imagine the horror on his face, the uneasiness with which he'll go forward.

I'm a fifteen-year-old girl, and I can't cope in the real world.

But I don't want other people to know that. I don't want *Adam* to know. I want to be equal, and it terrifies me I won't be enough for him, that I'm not enough for myself.

Deep breath. Look, he's smiling, his arms are curling around my waist, his fingers playing with the hem of my t-shirt. How can I question this? How can it be wrong when Adam makes me feel so invincible?

"You okay?" Adam shouts above the music.

I nod because words might betray me.

"Do you want to go?"

I nod again, with relief this time.

The roads are empty on the way home. There's no colour apart from the dull orange glow of the streetlights resting on the mist, appearing sepia like an old photograph. There's no colour in the real world.

Adam's in my kitchen wearing just his boxers and a fleece of mine which is too large for me and slightly too tight for him.

"Bagels or toast?"

"You choose."

My head is exploding with so many thoughts pulling me in different directions: shrill, obnoxious ones which demand my attention, shy and quiet ones peeking out with a raised hand. They mimic you, Cat, but I can't make out what they're trying to say.

"Bagels. The cinnamon ones." He carries a plate piled up and the butter glistens in the overhead light. "Come to bed?"

"Can we..." I stop. I don't know what I was going to say. It was there, on the edge of my consciousness, but it disappeared and left me floundering. I smile and follow.

I nibble half the bagel, sucking the butter, pulling raisins with my teeth. I cuddle into Adam, my head resting on his chest rising and falling as he breathes, listening to the echo of his heartbeat.

And I'm crying. Why am I crying? You know, Cat, don't you? You feel the dull ache in my stomach, the pressure squeezing my lungs.

"Adam... I can't..." I stare at the wall and frown. It's almost there, this thing I should say. "I love you. You know that, right?"

He says nothing. He brushes hair from my face with his other hand, away from my tear-damp face.

"I can't..."

He doesn't let me finish. His arms wrap tightly around me. He kisses the top of my head, combing his fingers through my hair, and he dips his head to kiss my forehead and my nose and my lips. And we don't move until morning.

***

In my world, when Rachel Carr walks into my maths class on that glassy late October day, she sits beside someone else. I get the fractions answer wrong, and of course I'm ridiculed. But I get over it; people forget. I lose weight the summer I take my GCSEs and find friends during my A-levels—not because I'm thinner, as I'd always assumed, but because I find confidence

I never had before. A switch is flicked, and I'm accepted—more than that, I'm liked. *Not* conforming becomes the norm, and I fit in without trying. I find a talent—and a love—for drama, and take roles in *My Fair Lady, Grease,* and *Cat on a Hot Tin Roof.*

A boy called Rob, who's been in my classes every year since Year 7, asks me out. We dance together when we receive our exam results and cry when we go our separate ways: Rob on gap year travels, me to university. I meet someone else. We dance together when we finish our degrees and cry when I remain in Cardiff and he moves back home.

I meet someone else at my first job as a journalist for a national newspaper, which is nice, but not serious. And I spend time alone, a single woman in a small city, doing anything I want and having fun.

When I meet Adam, a hundred miles, a hundred lifetimes away, I ask him out. Because he's my destiny, and our first date feels like we've known each other forever. We marry two years later; we have two sons. We are happy.

In my world, it's me who never wakes up from that formidable cocktail of pills and cheap rum; it's my shattered, wasted body Rachel's mother stumbles over in her haste to reach her own comatose daughter. It's my grave which sits untended among weeds; my parents' marriage that dissolves under the strain of it all while I'm helpless to stop it, wishing things had been different.

Because I didn't want to die, didn't crave it; had never even thought of death until Rachel Carr walked into my classroom, one glassy late October day, and sat beside me.

Her destiny, perhaps.

Maybe you were never heartless or devious, Cat. Maybe you were just Rachel all along, a perfectly normal girl who had challenges, who aspired to be dangerous and different, to stand out from the crowd, but didn't know how; a girl who grew up and met Adam in different circumstances, a hundred miles, a hundred lifetimes away.

In my world, I never existed.

I'm a dream, a fragment, a passing thought. I'm someone's imaginary friend. Rachel's perhaps—guiding her through the unrelenting pain that she couldn't navigate by herself, offering solace when no one else could.

My mother and father are forging different, happier lives— possibly together, probably apart.

Somewhere in the world, Adam is in love and content. He drinks Champagne at the top of the Eiffel Tower on his honeymoon and watches the sun set. He briefly feels disorientated, as though he shouldn't be there with *this* woman, slightly out of step with reality. He feels the brush of someone's hand, a shadow behind him. But it passes.

And I'm a fantasy, a wisp. I'm a butterfly on the breeze. I'm a long way from here.

Acknowledgements

This novella is a reissue of a book released in 2012 by Vagabondage Press. I'd like to offer my heartfelt thanks to Fawn, Nanette, and everyone at Vagabondage for believing in Julia's story as much as I did. I'm excited to take her on this next step of her journey, but I'll always remember where she began.

I want to thank my husband, Peter, who gives me his unwavering support. When I asked his opinion on this project, he simply said, "Yes." For many years he's been my rock – back in 2012, and still today.

Since the first edition of this book, authors are much more aware of the issues within our pages which might have an effect on our readers. If the issues raised in this book affect you, please contact PAPYRUS Prevention of Young Suicide (UK) or SAVE Suicide Awareness Voices of Education (US).

About the Author

Annalisa Crawford lives in Cornwall, UK, with a good supply of moorland and beaches to keep her inspired. She lives with her husband, and canine writing partner, Artoo. Her two sons have flown the nest, but still like a mention.

Annalisa writes dark contemporary, character-driven stories, with a hint of paranormal.

She is the author of four short story collections, and her novels Grace & Serenity (July 2020) and Small Forgotten Moments (August 2021) are published by Vine Leaves Press.

For more information visit
www.annalisacrawford.com

www.ingramcontent.com/pod-product-compliance
Lightning Source LLC
Chambersburg PA
CBHW031006210726
48290CB00007B/2501